The Fugitive

The Fugitive / *Forty Ali Babas and a Thief*
ISBN: 978-1-945307-14-0

Book compilation and design by Rodney Schroeter.

The Silver Creek Press
PO Box 334
Random Lake WI 53075-0334

rschroeter@silentreels.com

The Fugitive

SCP Tête-Bêche
Book 1

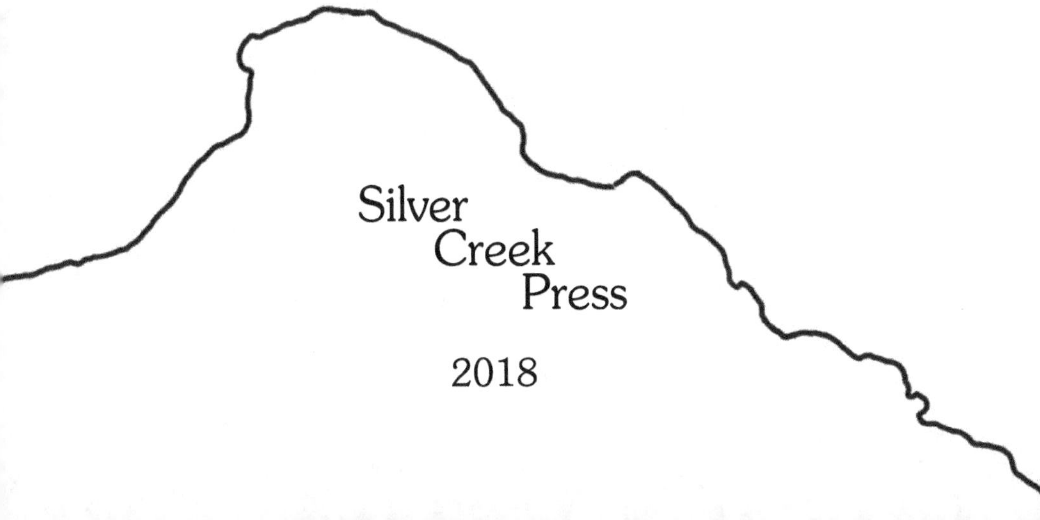

CHAPTER I.

IN PERIL BY THE JORDAN.

A LONG, tortuous stream—a creek rather than a river—mud-colored, swift, turbulent; and in a cleared space along the western bank a group of three white tents. In front of the largest tent lounged an elderly woman and a man.

"And this is the Jordan!" the woman was saying as she eyed the turgid yellow river with disappointment. "I had pictured it as so different."

"You and most of the rest of us Americans, Mrs. Sharpe, get your ideas of Holy Land scenes from pictures painted by people who were never nearer Syria than Sandy Hook," rejoined the florid, stout old gentleman who sprawled on the grass at her feet.

"It is only a few of us who are lucky enough to see the real thing," he went on, "and even then we are apt to feel disappointed until we grasp the subtler side of it all. Personally, I'm glad I came. I enjoy every hour of my stay."

"You aren't the only member of the party who is extracting wholesale enjoyment," replied Mrs. Sharpe, lowering her voice and nodding significantly toward two men and a girl who were coming up the path from the river bank toward the tents. "Your niece, Miss Farrar, ought to be happy with all the attention she is receiving. Look at her, dividing her favors impartially between young Mr. Mohun and Sir Arthur. I confess to a lively interest in that triangular love affair."

"'Love affair' is hardly the word for it, I hope!" retorted the major testily. "May has a good, level head on her shoulders, and she's not foolish enough to take too seriously the attentions of chance traveling acquaintances.

"But," he added under his breath, "if she *does* fall in love with either of them, I hope it won't be with that young human beanpole with a title tied to it. Mohun is a hundred per cent the better man of the two."

The trio of young people had drawn too near to permit Mrs. Sharpe to answer. The kind old lady smiled up at the flushed, eager face of the tall girl who stood before her, and her gaze passed on with scarcely less friendliness to a stalwart, bronzed youth of medium height who stood on May's left hand and who appeared to have been arguing hotly with her on some topic.

The third member of the trio, a long, lank youth with a perpetual smile, colorless hair, and a nose three sizes too large for the rest of the small, sallow face, almost justified at first glance the major's unkind description, "A human beanpole with a title tied to it."

Yet Sir Arthur Cole, Baronet, was regarded by many as a decidedly desirable *parti,* and he himself thoroughly concurred in this opinion. It was evident he had been an onlooker rather than a participant in the discussion between Mohun and May Farrar, as he looked uncomfortably from one to the other and seemed anxious to lead the talk into some other channel.

"Uncle Jack," cried the girl, partly in fun, partly in vexation, "will you kindly explain to Mr. Mohun that if I need any advice as to my conduct I can come to you for it without troubling him?"

Mohun reddened under his bronzed skin as the major and Mrs. Sharpe looked at him in quizzical inquiry.

"If I've interfered with Miss Farrar's wishes," he began, "it was merely for her sake. Not for my own amusement. There is an old raft down at the shore. Miss Farrar wants to take my groom, Imbarak, and cross to the other side of the river."

"Well, why shouldn't she?" asked the major. "If the raft will hold them both?"

"That's just what I said!" exclaimed May.

"Because," replied Mohun gravely, "Imbarak tells me the other side is unsafe; that boars have occasionally been found in the thickets there; that the footing is treacherous; and that snakes are not unheard of in the patches of marshy ground. But if Miss Farrar really wants to cross, and if you think it safe, sir, I shall be glad to cross with her."

"So shall I," broke in Sir Arthur. "I'd be jolly glad to escort her anywhere. But if there's really danger, hadn't she better—"

"I don't want the escort of either of you, thanks!" retorted May with pretty willfulness. "I mean to be the first of my party to explore the east bank of the Jordan. Imbarak doesn't count. He says he understands rafts, and he can shoo away any boars. Besides, I've got this"— and she drew a small revolver from her pocket—"in case of snakes or—"

"If the snakes would only stand behind you they'd fall ready victims to your skill as a markswoman," laughed the major; "but of course you can go if you choose to. I've no patience with this talk of peril in the Orient.

"Syria is as safe as Jersey City. Every traveler knows that. Robbers, dangerous wild animals, and fanatics were all cleared out years ago. But Americans who come to the Holy Land like to pretend they are in an atmosphere of peril.

"It disgusts me, this continual harping on danger, danger, danger! Cross the Jordan if you want to, May; if you're sure Imbarak understands handling a raft. The worst danger you'll incur will be a spill into the water. And I think there are enough men here to rescue you if you do upset."

"But," protested Sir Arthur, "it would be beastly cold to tumble into the Jordan in winter. Do be careful, Miss Farrar."

There was a laugh at the baronet's serious tone, and a second laugh at the blank stare of surprise. Then, with a triumphant glance at Mohun, May Farrar left the group and beckoned up a small, wiry man in native garb.

"Imbarak," she called loudly enough for Mohun to hear, "get the raft ready and we will cross now."

"*I-o-a, sit*" (Yes, madam), responded the little brown man with alacrity, "but Mr. Mohun? Does he say I can go? I am *his* groom."

May turned impatiently toward Mohun, too proud to ask his leave. But he saved her the trouble by nodding curtly at Imbarak and then turning his back on them both.

"You spoke a few minutes ago, sir," he said to the major, "about the absence of danger in Syria. You were partly right, of course. But in all Eastern countries, so I have read, nothing is certain except uncertainty. And Syria is no exception.

"Of course the Bedouins no longer as a rule commit robberies openly in the more settled districts here, nor do Moslem fanatics openly kill Christians just to prove their piety. But Bedouins are still thieves at heart, and fanatics only await the chance to kill every Christian within reach. All that either Bedouins or fanatics need to make them as dangerous as of old is a word of encouragement from high quarters."

"But that word shall never be spoken. The Sultan of Turkey is—"

"The Sultan is a solitary, isolated man, struggling vainly to reform and build up a nation which ought to be the richest on earth and which is the poorest. The pashas grind down the peasantry and townfolk and send lying reports to their masters of the country's condition. The Christians in Syria, especially in Damascus, where we are planning to go next week, have prospered under the just laws of the present Sultan, and the local Mohammedans are discontented.

"There's a fairly well-defined rumor that the authorities at Damascus are scared at the growing hatred against the Christians, and that a clique of nobles there are almost openly advocating a massacre and a general looting of Christians' property. The nobles have their eyes on the 'Unbelievers'' wealth, and also want to make themselves popular with the rabble. The authorities fear the influence of the nobles with the Sultan, and therefore they dare not crush the threatened revolt with an iron hand. Things are getting serious up there, I hear. Perhaps it might be wiser to postpone—"

"Postpone our trip there?" cried the major, who had listened with incredulous impatience. "My boy, you're talking arrant nonsense! We're living in the latter half of the nineteenth century and under the protection of the American flag. Massacre? Rot!"

"But it's true that fanatics from all parts of Islam are flocking to Damascus; and Bedouins from the Syrian Desert, and—"

"If you're afraid to risk your life there, Ralph," said the major disgustedly, "stay in the safer neighborhood of Jerusalem. We should be sorry to lose your society, of course, but we don't want you to die of fright.

"Why, man alive, do you suppose I'd take my niece to Damascus if there was an atom of danger? Or that I'd advise the rest of our party to go there with us if it were not perfectly safe? Absurd!"

"I think you know that I don't fear for myself," said Mohun, rising from the deck chair into which he had thrown himself, "but as to safety—well, as Sir Richard Burton once said, 'There can be no real security in the lands darkened by the Shadow of the Prophet.'"

He strolled away toward the river bank, where he stood watching Imbarak deftly guiding the raft through the swirl of yellow waters toward a wide strip of white sand on the opposite bank.

"I'm sorry I spoke so harshly to the boy," said the major, looking after him. "I shouldn't have pretended to doubt his courage, for if I'm any judge of men he's as plucky and as square a chap as ever I saw. But his talk of danger riled me. I trust, madam," he went on, turning to Mrs. Sharpe, "that *you* are not alarmed at the prospect of going to Damascus with us?"

"Why, to be frank with you, I *am*," replied the old lady. "I'm a little timid by nature I suppose, and all this talk of fanatics and Bedouins and the 'Shadow of the Prophet' frightens me. But," she added brightly, "I'm going all the same. It will be my only chance, for I must return to Boston next month."

"So soon? I thought you were to stay on this side of the Atlantic until summer."

"I was. But my mail, that M. Gelat sent on from Jerusalem to-day, has altered my plans."

"No bad news, I hope?"

"Very bad, I fear. But it's a longish story, and I won't bore you with it."

"Nothing you tell me, madam, could possibly bore me," and there was a note of real feeling in the pompous tones that brought a faint flush to her withered cheek. "I beg that you will let me know if I can be of assistance in any way."

"Thank you, major. I appreciate your words more than I can say. My news, in brief, is that the great banking house of Warren & Co., of Boston, is in grave danger."

"You don't say so! I thought it was one of the most solidly established houses in America. Mark Warren, the president of the bank, was a chum of mine in Yale. I haven't seen him for ten years, but up to that time we were like brothers. Poor old Mark!"

"You are wasting your sympathy on him if the reports in my letter are true. It is thought that he or some member of his firm has squandered in speculation a large sum of money entrusted to the bank's keeping. All my little fortune is involved, and if the bank fails I—But don't let us think of that. I only mention it to explain why I must cut short my visit to the East. My letter was from a lawyer whom I know. It was delayed three weeks by the cholera quarantine at Port Said. I

should have received it nearly a month ago. At the time it was writ-
ten the story of the defalcation was still hushed up. But it is probably
public by now, and the bank may have gone to pieces for all I know.
Oh, if there were only some means of getting news! I—"

A cry from the farther bank, an answering shout, and the sound
of a plunge into the water, brought them both to their feet. Sir Arthur
Cole, who had strolled farther up the clearing, also turned, and all
three ran toward the bank.

There one glance explained the entire situation to the major's eyes,
sharpened as they were by many campaigns and surprises.

May Farrar and Imbarak had beached their raft on the east bank
and had started across the wide strip of white, moist sand toward the
higher ground. They had not taken a dozen steps when both had sunk
to the knees in the treacherous footing.

The groom had at once recognized the nature of the danger and
had tried to throw himself face downward on the sand, but his feet
were already too deeply embedded. May, not comprehending, had
struggled to free herself, with the inevitable result that she sank at
once to the waist in the white, shifting sands.

Imbarak's agonized face and his gasp of "Quicksands!" told her the
full story of her peril, and she cried wildly for aid.

Ralph Mohun, on the opposite bank, had for the moment turned
his eyes from the newly-landed explorers and was watching a gnarled
tree floating down-stream, but May's cry had scarcely reached his ears
when his coat, waistcoat and shoes were tossed off and he had leaped
into the icy waters of the Jordan.

With long, overhand racing-stroke he battled his way across the
swift stream, aiming for a point higher up in order to counterbalance
the effect of the current. Each stroke carried the upper half of his body
out of the muddy torrent.

Logs, branches and other floating debris buffeted him cruelly, but
he managed to keep his head clear of any of these obstacles, and each
cleaving stroke carried his muscular body nearer the quicksands.

The major, Sir Arthur and the servants, meantime, were rushing
aimlessly along the western bank in the vain search for a boat, and
bellowing foolish advice to the imperiled girl.

Imbarak had ceased to struggle, and his brown face took on a stoical, dull look, the intense fatalism of the East having laid hold upon his brain and nerves.

May, however, her straining eyes fixed on the alternately rising and sinking face of the swimmer, continued to struggle fiercely as she felt the quicksands drawing her deeper and deeper into its grip.

The Jordan, at no point wide, is barely two hundred feet from bank to bank at the spot where tourists usually camp. It was thus but the work of a minute for so expert a swimmer as Ralph Mohun to reach the place where the raft was beached. Scrambling on it, he bent his full strength to the task of ripping off the broad boards that formed its deck.

The raft was old, the nails rusty, and in a moment he had torn four of the boards free. Throwing them, two by two, upon the sands he sprang across them to where May, buried almost to the shoulders, awaited him. The wide surface of the planks withstood the suction of the treacherous sand.

Luckily, in quicksand it is almost as easy to draw forth an object embedded as it is for that object to sink in. Therefore a single tremendous pull of Ralph's powerful arms sufficed to lift May from the moist, quaking grave into which she had so nearly lost her life, and to place her, trembling and exhausted, on the planks beside him.

His arm still encircled her, and for one brief, pregnant instant rescuer and rescued looked into each other's eyes.

In that look a knowledge, a wonderful certainty, passed from one to the other.

Through her exhaustion the girl felt a wave of color surge to her face. The man's eyes glowed and darkened. Neither spoke.

A cheer from the little group on the opposite bank and the spell was broken. Picking her up lightly in his arms, Ralph Mohun carried May to the wreck of the raft, set her down there, and bounded back to where Imbarak waited.

Wresting the luckless Syrian from the clinging sands less gently than he had lifted May from them, Mohun deposited the limp, nerveless body on the planks.

"Come!" he said sharply. Brace up! Help me move these planks back to the raft. Step on the next one and then, lift this one you're on now. We'll need them."

Dully the native obeyed. He had been too near death to realize clearly his unexpected deliverance.

Working mechanically under Mohun's orders, he gained the strip of safer sand where the raft lay and set to work at his task of repairing the rude vessel.

Five minutes later the three were on the west bank again, May crying quietly in Mrs. Sharpe's arms, and Mohun looking very foolish as he received the thanks of the much-flustered major.

"You showed pluck, my boy!" the older man was vociferating, "and what is better, you showed presence of mind. It was a proof that—"

"That there may still be a few dangers even in Syria?" queried Ralph innocently, and the major's mingled resentment and gratitude strangled the reply in his throat.

But a diversion occurred to end the embarrassing situation. Imbarak, the groom, who had stood stupidly staring across at the quicksands, suddenly turned and walked up to the tourists.

Slowly unwinding his dirty white turban, the Syrian laid it at Mohun's feet. Ignorant of Eastern customs, Ralph did not realize that this is the world-old oriental form of vowing eternal allegiance—not until the groom's words enlightened him.

"*Howaji,*" said Imbarak simply, "I am your dog. By the tombs of my fathers, by the sword of the Prophet, I lay my life forever at your feet. When the hand of death was on me, you lifted me to life again. Another would have saved the *sit* and would have forgotten the servant. My life is yours. I say it—*I, Imbarak Abou-Najib.*"

The quiet simplicity with which he spoke robbed the words of much of their melodramatic effect, yet, with the Anglo-Saxon hatred of demonstrativeness, Mohun looked and felt supremely uncomfortable as he answered lamely.

"Oh, that's all right. Glad to have been able to do you a good turn. Let the matter drop there!"

He walked away, leaving the native to pick up and resume his turban and to mutter guttural prayers of gratitude in his own dissonant Arabic tongue.

CHAPTER II.

A SURPRISE.

FOR two days longer the party remained encamped beside the Jordan, making little horseback trips to the near-by ruins of ancient Jericho; to the salt plains at the northern end of the Dead Sea; to that weird, uncanny body of water, the Dead Sea itself; and to the sites of the Cities of the Plain.

The whole valley of the Jordan is full of wonders of nature and of historical and religious interest. The Americans, with the exception of two of their party, enjoyed the experience to the full.

These two exceptions were Ralph Mohun and May Farrar. And the reason for their lack of interest in outside environment was easy to understand.

When Ralph Mohun had chanced to meet Miss Farrar and the major, through having a seat at their table at Shepheard's Hotel in Cairo a month before, both uncle and niece had taken an instant liking to him. On hearing that he was on his way to the Holy Land they begged him to join their party. Hesitatingly he consented.

A frank friendship of rapid growth had sprung up between the young fellow and May, and had, unconsciously on both sides, ripened into a deeper feeling of whose nature and comprehensiveness both had for the first time become aware in that one moment of rescue on the quicksands.

But since then, to May's surprise and chagrin, the man appeared to avoid her. He seldom addressed her directly, and evaded all chances of a tête-à-tête.

At first May fancied this attitude on his part might be accidental, and she was secretly grateful for the respite wherein she might adjust her mind and heart to this new and wonderful emotion which, springing into life in one moment, now filled and swayed her whole being.

But before the party turned their faces toward Jerusalem on the morning of the third day, May Farrar could no longer doubt that Mohun's new coldness of manner and actual avoidance of her were intentional.

That he was unhappy she could plainly see. That his disquiet had to do with her she readily guessed.

Woman-like, and conscious of freedom from offense, she was too proud to seek an explanation or to try to force her society on a man who was obviously seeking to avoid it.

Thus it was that with unseeing eyes the two young people gazed on scenes fraught with the world's most marvelous history and most sacred religious associations.

It is a day's journey by fairly easy stages from the Valley of the Jordan to Jerusalem. Part of the route lies over a rough road laid in the days of Roman rule, and little improved in the past nineteen centuries, and part lies over a mere narrow, rock-girt path where carriages cannot pass and where horsemen must ride single file.

The first portion of the journey is through shaded orchards of olive, orange and lemon trees laden with fruit and flower. The latter part is over a mountainous, barren, desolate tract where dull-gray rock and duller brown earth blend into a monochrome of dreariness.

"It is like a Land of the Dead," commented Mrs. Sharpe to the major, who rode beside her palanquin.

"It *is* a land of the dead," he answered gravely. "A land whose glory is departed. But there are more holy memories roused by the outlines of these barren hills and by the very dust of these roads than by all the beauties of the rest of the world.

"This land is the cradle of our faith. I feel that with every step I take I am treading on holy ground. I only wish," he added with a sigh, "that I could instil a little feeling of the sort into our young people here."

He indicated with his head Sir Arthur and May, who were riding together a hundred yards in advance of their elders, laughing and chatting gaily.

"Youth is youth!" responded Mrs. Sharpe oracularly, "but evidently the 'triangular love affair' is no longer triangular. Where is Mr. Mohun? Have he and May had a tiff?"

"I hope not," said the major, turning in his saddle to locate the missing swain, "for I like the boy. I'd be sorry if May had trifled with his heart to any serious extent. He's too good a chap for her to torture. There he is now, riding with Imbarak nearly half a mile behind us.

What ails the lad? On the journey from Jerusalem to the Jordan he never left May's side."

"I wouldn't worry. Probably some silly misunderstanding such as young people enjoy. You seem fond of Mr. Mohun. Are you prepared to welcome him as a nephew-in-law?"

"Well, I'd hardly say that. You see I know so little of him. We met him accidentally in Cairo and liked him and insisted on his joining us. He is from Boston, is recently out of Harvard, and is spending a year in travel before settling down to business. That is all he has told me about himself. He seems to have plenty of spending money and plenty of leisure, and from his manner I can see he is a gentleman by birth and breeding.

"That's all I really *know* of him. If he and May come to an understanding it will of course be my duty as her uncle and guardian to make strict inquiries as to his family, finances, antecedents, etc. But it has struck me that for the past day or so he and May don't seem as fond of each other's society as of old—ever since he helped her out of the quicksands, in fact. Queer, isn't it? But young Cole is getting his innings on account of it."

"I've lived in and around Boston all my life," said Mrs. Sharpe reflectively, "and I know, by name or personally, nearly every family of any account in the whole city. But I recall no name such as Mohun. Nor, though I've questioned him once or twice, can I make him speak of any acquaintances in Boston. Besides, I've noticed that though we have all been together for more than a month he has never received any mail. Not a single letter.

"Nor have I ever seen him writing so much as a postcard in the hotel writing-rooms on steamer-days. It is none of my business, and I suppose I am a prying, spying old woman, but all this strikes me as odd. May I advise you, in case affairs *do* come to a head, to make very strict inquiries before trusting that dear little girl's life and happiness into his care?"

"You may count on me," said the major stiffly, "but I believe and earnestly hope that you are mistaken—if I am any judge of faces. And yet all you say of his peculiarities strikes *me* as odd now that I think it over. Well, let's hope it will turn out all right. But I'm sorry to have a doubt of Ralph planted in my mind. For, as I said, I'm fond of the boy.

Let us talk of something else, please."

Meantime Mohun had some time before made a pretext of dismounting and examining his saddle-girth, with Imbarak's assistance, and had thus allowed himself to drop behind the rest of the little cavalcade.

"Well," he said to the groom as he remounted, "you asked me to drop back. What did you want?"

"To speak to you in private, *howaji*. I may not get a chance at the hotel."

"If it is any more of that nonsense about your gratitude—"

"It is not, *howaji*. But it is because of that gratitude that I speak. May I proceed?"

The groom, like many another Moslem in impoverished circumstances, had as a boy taken advantage of the universal opportunity which the American college at Beirut offers to natives to secure an occidental education. He therefore spoke English with an almost imperceptible accent, and while clinging to Moslem faith and Islam conditions had acquired as much occidental learning as the average American grammar school graduate.

"Go on," assented Mohun. "What is it you wanted to tell me?"

"What I say I must ask you to regard as secret, sir. Have I your promise?"

Mohun nodded carelessly, his mind and eyes on a trim, slender figure in close-fitting riding-habit half a mile ahead.

"I wish to warn you, *howaji*, not to go to Damascus, and to beg you to prevent your friends from going."

"Then you believe this rumor of an uprising against the Christians?" asked Ralph with new interest.

"*Believe* it? I *know* it is true. The *Ukh-ul-Rasoul* (Brotherhood of the Prophet), of which I am a member, has sent word to Damascenes in every part of Syria to 'come home to the feast.' I am of Damascus. My mother lives there in the Street of the Mehdan."

"And you mean to say that this fraternal crew of cut-throats is actually sending out invitations to its members to come and cut Christians' throats? It is the most—"

"Do not judge, *howaji!* You are of the West, we of the East. You cannot understand. The *Ukh-ul-Rasoul* is but one of many guilds in

Damascus that have suffered from the Sultan's weak toleration of the Christians. The nobles are behind us. The *serail* (local government) knows but cannot prevent. There will be killing and plundering and burning. I, whose life is yours, warn you to stay south here where there is safety."

"And you actually intend to join in this slaughter?"

"I? No, *howaji*. I have learned the education of the Christian; I have seen that he is a good man and not a sorcerer, as my brethren believe. While I do not embrace his creed, I honor and revere it. I shall take no part in the 'feast.'"

"Yet you will keep silence and let innocent men—perhaps even women and children—be murdered?"

"It is kismet, *howaji*. It is fate. Their lives are in the hollow of Allah's hand. It is not for one to speak. Besides," he added, a practical note creeping into his apathetic voice, "my brethren would kill me with most unpleasant tortures if I betrayed them."

"We will not go to Damascus. I can answer for that. I suppose I ought to thank you, but—"

"The major is calling, *howaji*. Shall we catch up with the rest? "

Putting their wiry Syrian ponies to a gallop, they swept past the baggage mules laden with tents and chests, breasted the rise of the hill, and joined the tourists who were awaiting them.

Mohun tried to laugh off the major's remonstrances at his long absence, but his mind was busy with plans for preventing the proposed visit to ancient Damascus.

They rode into Jerusalem, tired, dusty and hungry, at nightfall. Mohun lingered for a word with Imbarak as the party dismounted in front of the Grand Hotel. The others passed on into the terrace reception-room.

"Any new arrivals since we left, landlord?" asked Sir Arthur as the portly host greeted them on the threshold.

"Only one, sir," replied the boniface; "an American gentleman—Mr. Zenas Shattuck, of Boston, U. S. A."

"Another fellow-citizen of yours, Mrs. Sharpe," the major was beginning gaily, when a man who had been standing in the center of the wide room slouched forward toward them.

He was long rather than tall, lean to emaciation, with enormous hands, feet and ears, and a wrinkled, grayish face, in whose narrow eyes and thin-lipped mouth a half-humorous shrewdness and a tremendous fund of latent energy seemed to dwell.

His keen glance swept the group and there was a suppressed look of disappointment on his leathery face as he ended the scrutiny.

"Heard my name mentioned," he said in an unmistakable "Down-East" drawl. "Let me make myself acquainted. I'm Zenas Shattuck, of—"

He paused and, turning suddenly, walked up to Ralph Mohan, who was just entering the room.

"I want you, young man," he said, laying his hand on the newcomer's shoulder.

Ralph spun around as though galvanized by the touch. His eyes rested on Shattuck with a sort of horrified fascination as the latter opened his thin lips to speak again.

But the words never left them. For, shaking off the momentary apathy of amazement, Mohun drove his left fist full into the other's face.

The long, lean man reeled backward with the velocity of a catapult, caromed against a table and tumbled heavily to the floor, upsetting a chair and a bric-à-brac-covered taboret in his fall. Before the prostrate victim could make a move to rise, before the amazed spectators could move or speak, Ralph Mohun with a single bound had reached the long French window leading out into the hotel gardens.

He tugged fiercely at the knob, then, putting his shoulders to the sash, burst the stout fastenings and leaped out into the darkness, a shower of glass clattering to the polished floor behind him.

Zenas Shattuck, revolver in hand, sprang through the wrecked window in hot pursuit.

CHAPTER III.

IN THE GARDEN OF SORROWS.

IN speechless astonishment the four tourists looked from one to another of their number, each seeing reflected in the nearest face the blank amazement of his own.

Cole was the first to break silence.

"Our friend Mohun seems to be—er—wanted, as the London bobbies say," he remarked dazedly. "What the deuce do you suppose he's done? That chap was a detective, I'll bet a fiver."

No one answered. Old Mrs. Sharpe, with feminine intuition, came closer to Miss Farrar and slipped an arm about the trembling girl's waist. She felt May's heart beating tumultuously and knew what that moment of suspense and shock must mean to her.

The embarrassing interval was broken by the return of Zenas Shattuck. He reappeared in the broken window-frame, muddy and bruised from several tumbles in the dark garden, his forehead bleeding slightly from Ralph Mohun's blow, and his whole aspect the picture of rough usage and disorder.

But the white blaze of rage in his little blue eyes, the wrath and pallor of his sallow, leathery face drew attention from mere details of costume.

"Did you catch him?" asked Sir Arthur with cheerful fatuity.

"Yes," snarled Shattuck savagely. "Of course I've got him. Here in my pocket. Any fool could see that."

"I—I suppose you're a detective?" faltered Sir Arthur, his Anglican mind groping for a hidden meaning in Shattuck's words.

"And I s'pose you're an Englishman," snapped Zenas; "and that shows how all-fired smart we both are."

"My friend Sir Arthur Cole did not intend to annoy you, Mr. Shattuck," said the major conciliatingly. "May I introduce myself? I am Major Crawford, of New York. You must pardon us for seeming inquisitive. You see, the man who has just escaped—through no fault of yours, I am sure—was a friend of ours. We have traveled for some time with Mr. Mohun, and—"

"Mr. *who?*" broke in the detective.

"Mr. Mohun—Mr. Ralph Mohun—the man—"

"So *that's* the name, is it?" growled Zenas.

"Why, what other? Do you mean he was traveling under an alias? "

"What I mean or what I don't mean is no concern of anybody's but mine and his. He's the man I'm after, all right. I've seen him often enough in Boston to know him. And I'll get him, too, even if he has given me the slip for the minute in that measly black garden out there.

Oh, I'll *get* him right enough!"

"Won't you tell us with what crime he is charged, constable?" asked Cole eagerly.

"No, I won't. Is that plain enough? It's none of your business. I've got a warrant for him and I'll get *him*. That's enough for you to know. If I'd had sense enough to communicate first with the chief of police here, instead of trying to be a smart Alec and play a lone hand, I'd never have let him slip."

"Do you know," babbled Cole, his monocle sweeping the group with benevolent triumph, "I've always had my suspicions of that Mohun. Always said to myself he was a queer Johnny. He'd never talk about himself, you know. Always distrust a chap that won't talk about himself. Now, *I* am *always* glad to talk about myself. I—"

"I'm afraid you were right, Mrs. Sharpe, in the suspicions you voiced today," said the major sadly. "I blame myself bitterly for being taken in by the fellow. And yet he seemed so straightforward, so gentlemanly!"

"Oh, don't talk of my wretched suspicions!" cried the poor old lady, casting a frightened glance at May, who, at her uncle's words, drew quietly away from the elder woman's protecting arm. "Don't talk of my wretched suspicions. I'm a bad-hearted old creature ever to have had such thoughts or to have spoken them. No doubt I was utterly mistaken. He may clear himself yet."

"Not he!" retorted the major with sorrowful conviction. "An honest man doesn't take to his heels when accused of crime or when accosted by a detective."

"But he may have lost his head."

"The man who had coolness and presence of mind enough to plan and carry out the rescue of May and the groom from the quicksand isn't likely to lose his head under a lesser emergency. No, no. I'm the last man who would have believed in his guilt if he hadn't given ample proof of it by running away."

"Always suspected him. Queer Johnny!" supplemented Sir Arthur, chuckling.

"If you'll excuse me, uncle," said May, "I think I'll go to my room. I'm very tired."

Zenas Shattuck looked keenly after the departing girl, noting the drooping lines of her figure and the set, hopeless look on her white face.

"The only one of the whole crowd that hadn't something to say against him," he muttered under his breath. "She'll bear watching."

* * * *

Early the following morning May Farrar came down into the terrace-room. The hotel was silent and the lower floors deserted in the gray of the Syrian dawn.

The girl had passed a sleepless, miserable night. The indoor air suffocated her.

She dreaded meeting her friends at the breakfast table, to hear their comments on her pallid complexion and black-ringed eyes. She felt that she must get out of doors—anywhere—by herself, to think matters over and to get a fresh grip on her shattered nerves.

Throwing a wrap about her shoulders—for the morning was as chill as the noon would be hot—she passed the sleeping porter and let herself out into the narrow street.

The thoroughfare was empty. On the roof of the gray Tower of David, directly opposite, a drowsy Turkish sentinel paced. Turning to the right, May walked rapidly toward the Jaffa Gate.

Even the walled confines of the Holy City seemed to oppress her. She wanted to be in the open country. Of Jerusalem's six modern entrances, the Jaffa Gate lies nearest to the Grand Hotel. The warder had just opened it for the day as May appeared.

The stolid Syrian stared open-mouthed at the unprecedented spectacle of a woman walking abroad alone and at dawn. Grumbling something to himself about the "madness of all *feringhi*" (foreigners), he watched her as she struck out with the free, graceful stride of the Anglo-Saxon pedestrian along the by-road that skirts the city's walls to the north.

Jerusilem long ago outgrew its walls, and the overflow has spilled in disorderly fashion to the west and south of the city, in the shape of all sorts of irregular, untidy structures from packing-box shanties to mud and stucco community buildings. To the north and the east the Holy City cannot spread.

The deep and precipitate sides of the valley, in whose center lies the Brook of Kedron and whose farther slope culminates in the Mount of Olives, cut off further building on the east, while a Mohammedan cemetery and irregularities of ground render growth almost equally impracticable on the north.

With this conformation vaguely in mind, yet half-unconscious as to her direction, May Farrar rounded the northwestern buttresses of the gray old walls and turned east toward Kedron.

Scavenger dogs prowled in the ditch at the base of the wall. An occasional peasant leading a donkey laden with wares for the morning's market passed May in the narrow road and eyed her in stupid wonder. But her self-possession and the absence of all furtiveness from her manner served almost as effectively as did the dumb misery in her face to avert insult.

She moved on unmolested, this slender, sad-eyed American girl, where a woman of any race save the Anglo-Saxon would have been subjected to a thousand perils.

Only once she paused. She was opposite the Damascus Gate and stopped to gaze for an instant at a low, skull-shaped hillock just north of the ditch-road.

The little hill was dotted by a number of graves and in its sides were the scars of abandoned quarries. The summit presented the one green spot in all that dreary, grayish landscape.

It was in a cave at the base of this hill that Gordon discovered the tomb and other evidences which led him and a large portion of the Christian world to identify the spot as the real Mount Calvary. The presence of Moslem graves on the sacred hill have prevented its demolition before the encroachment of building enterprises.

The sun, rising over the Mount of Olives, gilded the green crest of Calvary as the girl gazed reverently. She bowed her head and stood thus a moment in silence before hurrying on.

A long string of mangy, mouse-colored camels, laden with bales and led by a furry little gray donkey, was toiling up the steep hill leading from Kedron as May began her descent, and she stood aside to let the ugly brutes and their grinning, shouting drivers pass.

Then she picked her way along the stone-strewn dusty highway to the valley below. Later in the day the dried bed of Kedron Brook at this point would be alive with traffic, discordant with the yells of vendors, and infested by loathsome lepers and other more or less unsightly mendicants.

But now over the whole scene brooded the solemn peace and hush of the dawn. The Mount of Olives loomed up before her, somber and beautiful. About its lower slopes clustered olive orchards and the white walls of monasteries.

Breasting the slope, May checked herself to look in through the wide-open gates of a walled garden. Winding natural paths intersected the neglected, flower-sprinkled turf, and enormous gnarled ancient olive trees cast a soft shade along the reaches of swaying grass.

The whole enclosure breathed of peace, repose, silence.

Passing through the gateway, May Farrar entered the garden. Here for the first time her restlessness vanished. A mystic sense of calm crept over her.

The tension of the past twelve hours relaxed. Throwing herself face downward in the long, soft grass, the girl fell to sobbing softly. And with the tears came peace.

Above, in the gray-green foliage of the olives, birds were twittering. Far in the distance the voice of a *muezzin* (priest) calling the faithful to morning prayer came faintly to her ears. Voice after voice from the distant city caught up the call as from minaret to minaret the *muezzins* sent forth their sonorous, chanting summons:

"Allah-hu-Akbar! La Illah Illah Allah! Mahmoud Siadnah Rasoul Allah!"

A light step on the gravel path near by broke in on the girl's grief and she sprang hastily to her feet.

Before her, his face swathed in the folds of a brown silk *kafieh* (native headdress), stood a Syrian. Some distance behind him, in the gateway of the garden, a second native was waiting. May at a glance recognized the farther man as Imbarak, the groom.

Despite the *kafieh* which shrouded the face and the long-striped *abbieh* and *kumbaz* which muffled the figure of the nearer native, there seemed something familiar about his bearing.

"What—what do you want?" she faltered in English.

Then, as he did not answer her at once, she repeated still more nervously in French:

"*Que voulez-vous?*"

A shake of the head and the *kafieh's* folds fell away from the man's face.

"Ralph Mohun!" cried May incredulously.

Mohun, his bronzed face dyed to an even deeper shade of brown, his dark mustache shaved, his muscular figure disguised in the shapeless costume of a native Syrian of the better *fellaheen* class, might have walked unrecognized through a double line of his closest friends. But the eyes of love are keen, and at a glance May Farrar knew him.

Surprise was her first emotion, then followed a feeling of anger against the man who, all unworthy, had won her love and had caused her such suffering.

It was Mohun who spoke first.

"Imbarak supplied me with this dress," he began lamely enough, "and he got me the dye for my face. There are so few Americans in Syria that I would have been captured in a day if I hadn't disguised myself."

"Why do you tell me this?" she asked coldly, finding her voice at last. "It can be of no interest to me."

"I did not venture to hope it would interest you," he answered. "I only spoke of it to explain my odd appearance."

"It needed no explanation. But something else does. And that is your motive in addressing me after—after—"

"After last night's scene?" he supplemented. "You are right, Miss Farrar. My venturing to address you at all or to claim acquaintanceship with you under such circumstances surely requires an explanation. Believe me, it was not from an idle whim that I followed you here."

"On second thought, Mr. Mohun, I do not care to hear any explanation you may offer. Please don't detain me any longer. I must get back to the hotel."

But he barred the path. She looked at him in astonishment.

"I shall only detain you a moment," he pleaded, "and I must ask you to hear me out. I should not trouble you with any affairs of my own. Please believe that. But this concerns your own safety."

She stood still without replying, and he continued:

"The major intends to take you to Damascus in a day or two. He must not do so. This is imperative. Had I remained with your party, I should have found a means to prevent it. As it is, I can only appeal to you, for your own sake, not to go. There is the gravest sort of danger awaiting all Christians—native and foreign alike—at Damascus.

"I tried to make your uncle understand this, but he would not. He may believe *you*. If he does not, you must feign sickness or resort to any subterfuge to avert the trip. Your life and the lives of the whole party may hang on this.

"Oh, can't you see I would not have risked detection and capture by lingering near Jerusalem until this morning if it had not been necessary to give you this warning and if the warning had not concerned your very life?"

He spoke with an earnestness that for the moment carried conviction. Whether or not his warning was justified, May felt that he had indeed imperiled his liberty by remaining to deliver it. And a quick revulsion of feeling seized her as she looked up into his troubled, eager eyes.

"Mr. Mohun—Ralph," she exclaimed, laying her hand impulsively on the coarse sleeve of his *kumbaz*, "forgive me if I judged you too harshly. I was wrong to condemn you without a hearing. Tell me the truth about yourself. Perhaps I can help you."

A spasm as of pain twisted his brown, dyed face and a light sprang into his haggard eyes as he listened. He opened his lips to speak, then checked himself as if by a tremendous effort. The perspiration stood out on his forehead.

A terrible struggle seemed waging within him. But when he spoke again his tone was dull and hopeless; and his eyes were averted from the pleading, beautiful face upraised to his.

"I can tell you nothing," he said.

"But you don't understand!" she insisted. "I am ashamed of myself that I ever doubted you even for a moment. If you had stood your ground last night, *none* of us would have believed that wretched Yankee detective. Oh, *why* did you run away? It was so—so unlike *you*."

"I—I can tell you nothing!" he repeated dully.

"You *must!*" she cried, stamping her foot with pretty insistence. "Can't you see I'll believe whatever you say—that I'll *know* you're speaking the truth—that I *trust* you? All you have to say is 'I am innocent,' and—"

"I cannot say it."

The words were spoken so low that she scarcely caught their import. But the droop of the man's head, the utter misery and despair of his countenance went straight to May's tender heart.

She could not—would not—believe him the guilty wretch that his face, his bearing, his words implied. She made one final effort to break down his reserve.

"Ralph Mohun," she said more quietly, "I know little of the world as men see it—little of the temptations and pitfalls that beset a man. So it is not for me to judge you. But this I *do* know: if you have been led into any folly or lawless act—I will not believe you capable of *crime*—the only honest and manly course open to you is to go back and bravely face the consequences of that act; not to hide from its results. Do that, and whatever your punishment I for one will be proud to call you my friend and to help you by every means in my power."

She checked herself, for as she had spoken his face had gone ghastly white under its coat of tan.

With inarticulate murmur, his parched throat sought to form words of reply.

"You are suffering!" she went on with a thrill of quick sympathy in her hurried words. "It would make it easier for you to tell me everything. I might help you. The mouse set the lion free from the net, you know, and—"

The man had regained control of himself. His face was calm, his voice expressionless as he broke in:

"I need not tell you, Miss Farrar, that it would be sweet beyond words to me if I might confide in you—if, in other words, I might be cur enough to roll my own load of responsibilities upon your shoulders.

"But there are reasons which I cannot explain that forbid my taking advantage of such a chance, even could I bring myself to do so. I repeat I can tell you nothing, and unfortunately I cannot even act on your advice to give myself up. You will of course attribute this latter determination on my part to cowardice."

The cold, studied brutality of his tone struck the girl like a blow in the face, dampening her ardor, chilling her zeal in his behalf.

"Then," she said slowly, "am I to believe—?"

"You are to believe what you will," he replied, the same forced coldness and brutality in his voice. "I can neither confirm nor deny your belief. I have delivered the warning; now I will intrude on you no longer. I can only thank you for all your kindness to me, for the faith you have tried to have in me, for the only words of hope and kindness that I shall perhaps ever hear."

"You avoided me after you saved my life at the Jordan. Why?"

"I cannot tell you."

"Had I offended you in any way?"

"*You?* No! You could never offend me."

"Oh, why make a mystery of all this? Why not be honest with me? Isn't there enough suffering, enough sorrow in the world without needlessly causing more?"

"Enough sorrow and suffering?" echoed Mohun, with a mirthless laugh. "Oh, there's enough of both. If you came here to forget them, you chose a strange place for the purpose.

"Do you know," he added, his cynical tone changing to one of reverence, "do you know what garden this is?"

"No."

"It is Gethsemane!"

"Gethsemane?"

"The Garden of Sorrows. Was it by chance you came here?"

"Yes." She spoke with a certain awe, recalling the mystic feeling of surcease from pain that had stolen upon her the moment her feet had crossed the threshold of the enclosure.

"And now," resumed Ralph, after a pause, "I must go. I shall probably never see you again. There is much I would say to you if I had the right. But I cannot even ask you to think gently of me. So let us say good-by. I suppose you don't care to shake hands with me?"

The appeal in his tone, strangely enough, awakened her slumbering indignation.

"How can you ask it?" she said bitterly. "You imposed yourself on us, accepted our friendship and became a member of our party without stopping to consider the disgrace and mortification that might accrue to us when the exposure came and when we should be known as the dupes and associates of a felon.

"I have appealed to you this morning—lowering myself to plead with you as I never thought I could with any living person; I have begged you to be honest with me. You owed *that,* at least, to me and to all of us. You refuse.

"I have implored you to return and face the consequences of your act as any man with a spark of honesty and courage should. You refuse. I have no alternative but to believe the worst of you. Don't you know yourself that an honest man *could* not act as you are doing?"

"Yes," assented Mohun heavily, "I suppose he couldn't. And now, if you have quite finished, may I go?"

CHAPTER IV.

FROM PITY TO CONTEMPT.

THE reaction from May Farrar's burst of righteous anger had set in. She was half-inclined to beg his forgiveness for the harshness of her judgment. Yet had he not even now, by his reply, acknowledged the justice of that judgment?

The memory of his face as he had looked into her eyes when his strong arms snatched her from death in the quicksands recurred to her with vivid distinctness.

"I spoke cruelly," she said with impetuous haste. "I forgot for the moment that I owe you my life. I ask your forgiveness."

"There is nothing to forgive," he returned; "and if you feel you owe me anything for what happened at the Jordan you can at once cancel the debt and make me happier by forgetting the whole occurrence."

"I can never forget it," she faltered, instinct and logic warring within her, and with the usual result.

She sank on her knees in the deep grass, buried her face in her hands and broke into a passion of weeping.

"Don't! For God's sake, don't!" he implored brokenly. "I'm not worth it! I'm not worth it, I tell you!"

He bent with outstretched arms as though to gather her to his heart, but by a mighty effort at self-control forbore.

A strand of her gold-brown hair had become loosened and fell across her heaving shoulders, glinting and shimmering as the morning sunbeams danced through it.

Ralph Mohun dropped on one knee, lifted the stray lock reverently, unobserved by the weeping girl, and pressed it once, twice, thrice in silence to his lips.

Then he rose and said once more, in a voice that he strove in vain to render conventional:

"Good-by, Miss Farrar."

A quick patter of slippered feet along the gravel behind them caused Mohun to turn nervously and brought May to her feet.

Imbarak came hurrying toward them. *"Howaji!"* he cried, breathless with fear. "Hide yourself! It is too late to go out by the gate, and there is no other exit."

"What's the matter?" asked Ralph.

"That tall man! The detective you told me had crossed the seas to find you! He is coming. Hide!"

"Shattuck!" gasped Mohun in alarm.

"Yes. I saw a man in *feringhi* clothes standing in the valley. He seemed to be waiting for the *sit*. He was too far away for me to see his face, but he started this way just now as if he was tired of waiting, and then I recognized him. Hide, *howaji!* Ah, it is too late!"

A long shadow fell across the gateway, and Zenas Shattuck, looking even more emaciated and gray of face than on the previous night, slouched into the garden.

May Farrar glanced keenly at Mohun and read in his face a panic-fear that changed her grief to a quick contempt. That one human being should thus shrink in dread of another filled her with disgust and robbed her of her one remaining vestige of pity for the cowering man before her.

Meantime Shattuck, after one comprehensive look among the shadows of the garden, strolled forward to where May and the two men stood. He noted her attitude of repulsion toward the nearer of the two supposed natives.

"These heathens botherin' you, Miss Farrar?" he drawled as he came up.

Mohun cowered at the voice, raising his hands to his face as if expecting a blow.

But May, her eyes still fixed on him, noted that the gesture was made for the purpose of drawing one of the long silken ends of the *kafieh* across his face.

But Ralph's next move struck her dumb with astonished disgust.

Extending his lean brown hand humbly toward her, Mohun whined cringingly:

"*Baksheesh, sit! Baksheesh!*" in the true Syrian beggar accent.

"Gee!" vociferated Shattuck. "It does beat all how these dirty Eastern beggars can pester one! I s'pose he saw you come in here alone and thought he could scare you into giving him money.

"Here, you!" turning threateningly on the cringing Mohun. "Get out o' here! Git, before I break this umbrella over yer heathen head! What's he got his face all bundled up for, I wonder?" he added curiously, taking a step toward the supposed beggar.

May gasped. But Ralph, desisting from his plea to her, addressed himself to Shattuck, never faltering for a second before the other's shrewd scrutiny:

"*Baksheesh, howaji!*" he whined in raucous, coughing accents; "*Baksheesh! Abras! Abras!*" ("Alms! I am a leper! A leper!")

"What's he jabbering about now?" snorted Shattuck.

"If please," volunteered Imbarak in very broken English as he came forward; "if please, he say—"

"Who the deuce are you? Another beggar?" demanded Shattuck, eying the wiry groom with scant favor.

"I custodian of garden. Spik Inglese same as 'Mer'can. Dis man ask alms. He say he leper."

"Leper!" yelled Zenas in horror, startled out of his usual profound self-control. "I want to know! A real leper, eh? I've read a lot about 'em in books. Don't let him come near me. It may be contagious. Why does he cover up his face, though?"

"That the law, *howaji.* Leper can not show face. Law. He a—"

"He's coming up to me again!" snorted Zenas angrily. "Tell him to go away! Run him out o' here or I'll report you."

"Imshi, Abras!" ("Be off, leper!") shouted Imbarak obediently, and Mohun began to shuffle away, followed by the indignant custodian.

"Wait!" commanded May Farrar.

She had been doing some quick thinking. Mohun's deception had increased her contempt for him and had added fuel to her wrath.

That she should thus connive at a malefactor's escape seemed unfair, dishonest. If, on the other hand, there were any palliating circumstances in Mohun's mysterious guilt, further flight would but make his position worse. In a flash she resolved to expose him.

"Wait!" she repeated, speaking quickly before her just intention could weaken. "Mr. Shattuck, you have been deceived!"

CHAPTER V.

INTO THE LION'S JAWS.

"MR. SHATTUCK," repeated May, "you have been deceived. This man is not—"

The words, despite her resolution, died in her throat, as the supposed leper ceased his shuffling walk toward the gate and freedom. He halted and looked quietly at her from above the disfiguring folds of his *kafieh.*

"The man is not what?" asked Zenas in surprise at the interruption and impatient at her pause.

Imbarak had unostentatiously slipped a short, curved knife from his girdle and had moved between the detective and Mohun. The flowing sleeve of the groom's *kumbaz* promptly concealed the ugly looking weapon, but not before May had seen it. Meantime, Ralph stood motionless, his quiet, expressionless eyes still fixed on the girl who held his freedom or the detective's life in the hollow of her little hand. There was no appeal in his look, no fear; simply steady, inquiring intentness.

Yet, under that unflinching regard, May Farrar's indignation died, her resolution wavered, her sense of justice vanished.

"Well?" reiterated Zenas. "What were you going to say about that man?"

"I—I was going to say," replied Miss Farrar weakly, as she indicated Imbarak, "that he is not custodian of this garden. He is probably an accomplice of the—the beggar. So don't fee him if he shows you about the place."

"Fee him? Not I!" grunted Zenas. "Be off, the pair of you!"

Imbarak and Mohun silently turned and walked from the enclosure. At the gate Mohun halted and seemed about to look back, but Imbarak's hand was on his arm and the groom hurried him away.

"Will you please take me back to the hotel, Mr. Shattuck?" asked May. "I am very, very tired."

Two days later the little cavalcade of tourists, with their dragoman, servants, tents and luggage, started north, across the country, for Damascus. The major had somewhat hurried their departure from Jerusalem, knowing what painful associations that locality must bring to his niece's mind. By tacit consent, neither he nor Mrs. Sharpe referred to Mohun in May's presence, and after one brief, incisive *tête-à-tête* with Mrs. Sharpe, Sir Arthur Cole was also prevailed upon to maintain the embargo on Ralph's name.

May was outwardly as cheerful and bright as ever, but that her gaiety was forced and her interest feigned was patent in her restless eye and pale cheek.

She had seriously considered the warning conveyed to her by Mohun concerning the danger of the Damascus visit, and had even hinted to Major Crawford that it might perhaps be well to abandon the jaunt.

But the bluff old soldier's indignant scouting of the bare idea of any peril, and his confidence in the safety of an American citizen in any quarter of the civilized or even semi-civilized globe, overbore her feeble protests and at last stilled her fears.

The girl had well-nigh implicit confidence in her uncle's judgment, and that confidence had rarely been misplaced.

Mrs. Sharpe, who had also been timid because of the rumors of impending religious trouble in the north, also coincided at last with Major Crawford's views and consented to go. The lady's only regret in starting so soon was that the delays to the American mails still prevented her from learning the present condition of the great banking house of Warren & Son.

Her fortune was all in that Boston firm's hands, and since the brief letter which informed her that a large sum of money had been embezzled and that the firm was tottering, she had had no further news from home.

She resolved, therefore, to join in the trip to Damascus, remain in that city a few days, and then return to America by way of Beirut, the nearest seaport town.

The northward journey through beautiful Samaria, with its Devon-like scenery and age-softened ruins, and through Cana, Nazareth and Southern Galilee passed uneventfully. Each day they rode from morning till night along the crooked, rocky footpaths which the natives miscall roads, stopping at noon to lunch beside some Scripture-famed stream, in the shade of a gigantic *terebinth* tree or in the mossy ruins of some crusader castle, and halting at sunset to find their tents awaiting them.

The evenings were spent in song and talk around a roaring campfire, and they sank to sleep under the big Eastern stars to the distant howling of mountain wolves, to the laugh of marauding hyenas in the valleys below, and the distant snapping bark of jackals quarreling over carrion among the nearer foothills.

One day, after crossing a wide plateau, they came out on the summit of a precipitous hill at whose foot the blue waters of a mighty lake danced and glittered.

"The Sea of Galilee!" proclaimed the dragoman grandiloquently, and the party halted, silent, awed and admiring. Even Cole's cheerful idiocy found no voice, and the major quietly uncovered his gray head.

They encamped on the pebbly margin of the lake that night, midway between the yellow-walled, dirt-infested town of Tiberius and the ancient cluster of grass-choked monoliths that marks the sight of Capernaum.

As they sat about the fire after the evening meal a clatter of horses' hoofs broke in upon the gentle lapping of waves against the shore. Out of the gloom, into the radius of firelight, appeared a dozen mounted figures. The foremost dismounted and walked forward, saluting the foreigners with an easy grace that is a part and parcel of the oriental manner.

The newcomer was a swarthy, middle-aged man, in the baggy uniform of a Turkish cavalry officer.

"You command this party, sir?" he asked politely, addressing Major Crawford in French.

"I am in charge of these ladies," replied the major. "What do you wish? To see our passports?"

"No, sir. I am sure your passports are correct. May I speak with you alone?"

He drew the major out of earshot of the others, who looked nervously after the receding form of their protector.

"Well, sir?" said the major curtly.

He hated mystery and dreaded the long-winded, circuitous fashion in which the typical oriental usually leads up to whatever he has to say.

But he was destined in this instance to be pleasantly disappointed. The Turkish officer came straight to the point.

"I am from the barracks at Tiberius," began the Turk. "We have received orders to-day from our superiors at Damascus to turn back all foreigners—whether tourists or those traveling on business—who may be going north. I am most sorry to—"

"But what is the meaning of this?" blustered the major fiercely. "Our passports are in correct order. This is a time of peace. We carry no contrabands. I demand as an American citizen to be allowed to proceed."

"My heart is desolated, sir," said the Turk, bowing humbly and spreading out both hands in deprecation, "but you cannot proceed farther north. Our orders are imperative. No foreigners are to be permitted to enter Damascus or to proceed in that direction until—until certain expected events have occurred.

"We are the friends of your great country, we Turks. We desire no international complications. Therefore—"

"International complications!" the major snorted. "What on earth is the man talking about? Do you think I intend to stir up any complications, international or otherwise?

"We are simply going on a pleasure trip to see the oldest city in the world. And you come here in a high-handed fashion and order us to turn back. I refuse to turn back. I—"

"I am but obeying my orders, sir," pleaded the officer, "and I beg that you will be reasonable. You cannot go to Damascus."

"But why?"

"My orders gave no reason," answered the Turk evasively, "and my orders must be obeyed. I shall have to see that you turn back by to-morrow morning."

"But, if I insist on going forward?"

"Your servants, sir, are all of them servants of my august master, the *Padishah* (Sultan)," responded the officer. "Without them you cannot proceed. And not a man among them will stir a foot toward Damascus when they know that the Sultan's representatives in Syria forbid them to do so."

The major, through all his wrath, recognized the truth of this statement. He knew that no Mohammedan nor Christian native in his employ would dare disobey an order of the soldiery.

He was at a standstill, and for the moment he reflected on the advisability of giving up his plan.

But the ignominy of being forced to confess to the ladies of his party that he had been worsted by a baggy-trousered Turk was more than he could face. He did not connect the matter with Mohun's ear-lier words concerning the chances of a massacre, but attributed it to the red tape that swathes every move and act in the Sultan's domain. Thus from blustering he turned to pleading, but with the same result. At length he recalled the cynical yet true proverb of the East: "Every man has his price."

"*Effendi*," he said, addressing the officer in a less stormy tone, "I greatly admire that sash you wear. I wonder if you would part with it for fifty *mejidie* (about $44)?"

The officer drew back in pained surprise.

"*Howaji!*" he exclaimed. "You insult me! I am a man of honor. I—"

"Forgive me," said the major hastily. "It was a slip of the tongue. I should have said one hundred *mejidie*."

The officer glanced down at his cheap cotton sash.

"It cost me one hundred and fifty *mejidie*," he replied reflectively. "I hate to part with it. I—"

"Permit me," interposed Major Crawford, opening his pocket-book. "Permit me to offer you two hundred *mejidie*. And," he added as the other, with many protestations of undying gratitude, counted and pocketed the money, "may I ask you to continue, wearing the sash as a memento of me?"

"*Effendi*, your generosity is as the light of the prophet's eyes," murmured the Turk. Then, in a more businesslike tone: "Break camp before dawn and continue on your way to Damascus. I shall say that I missed your tents in the darkness. A pleasant journey to you!"

A more suspicious hearer than the major might have detected a note of malicious irony in those last words.

Major Crawford and the officer were strolling back toward the fire when the group of cavalrymen, who had remained mute and motionless in the background throughout the colloquy, suddenly exhibited signs of activity.

One of them called something in Arabic to the officer, who gave a curt order in response. The soldiers cantered off, widening out their squad until they formed a line of videttes from lake-edge to the bluffs at the landward extremity of the beach.

"What's the matter?" queried Major Crawford, as the officer lumbered into the saddle.

"One of my men heard two horses approaching at a gallop from the south," was the reply. "Night travel at such speed is not customary."

The sound of horses approaching rapidly along the lakeside road from the direction of Jerusalem was now plainly audible even to the less keen-eared occidentals. Soon two mounted figures loomed up, shadowy and grotesque in the gloom beyond the fire. The riders had, apparently, no intention of stopping at the tourists' camp, but continued their reckless gallop northward.

"*Uiguf!* (Halt!)" commanded the officer.

One of the two riders slackened his pace, but the other called over his shoulder in a drawling, nasal twang that broke strangely on the stillness of the Palestine night: "Come along, you blame heathen! What yer stopping for? We've got no time to waste!"

"*Halte-là!*" repeated the officer, this time in French, and as the foremost rider made no sign of having heard, two of the cavalrymen spurred across his path.

There was a struggle, a scraping of hoofs as the American's mount was pulled sharply to its haunches, and then the nasal voice drawled once more, with no tinge of excitement in it: "If this is a hold-up, I warn you heathens I'm armed and that I'll commence unlimbering my battery in a second if you don't let me go."

"It's that wretched detective!" growled the major.

Then, raising his voice, he called: "Hey, Shattuck! Those men are soldiers. They aren't brigands. You'll save trouble by yielding."

A grunt of disgust was all the reply vouchsafed, but the detective made no further resistance as the troopers led his horse within the glow of the firelight.

"This is late to be riding so fast, Mr. Shattuck," observed the major, forcing himself to speak civilly. "What are you doing here in Galilee? When I saw you last you were hunting in Jerusalem for—"

He stopped short with an uneasy glance at May, who sat, chin in hands, gazing into the fire and giving no sign that she had noticed the words.

"Hunting that slippery young cuss that gave me the slip?" finished Zenas. "Yes, I was. But I hear he's got clear of the country by taking ship from Jaffa. He got away from me, anyhow, and he may be half way to France by now, for all I know or care.

"But I thought while I was here in Palestine I'd take a look around on my own account and see some of the Bible sights I've read about. You see, I ain't likely ever to be in this part of the world again, and I may as well enjoy myself while I'm here.

"So I'm on my way to Damascus. City that St. Paul went to, you know. And—"

"Damascus?" broke in the officer in French, catching the one familiar word in Shattuck's speech. "Does your friend say he is on his way to Damascus?"

Summoning Shattuck's native servant, he began to question him sharply.

"This man says," continued the officer at last, addressing the major, "that the tall, thin American there hired him in Jerusalem and that they are on their way to Damascus. He says his employer speaks no French. I, alas! know no English. Please tell him, therefore, of the unfortunate order I have received which forces me to forbid him to go on to Damascus. Please tell him he must turn back."

Not without secret amusement Crawford translated the message.

He disliked the cadaverous, drawling Bostonian, and desired for his own sake as well as for May's that the man who had indirectly caused them so much unhappiness should not be thrown further into their society on the road nor in Damascus.

He rather relished the anticipation of Zenas' discomfiture, but he was in no way prepared for the outburst of almost childish anger wherewith Shattuck received the news that he could not continue his journey.

"It's an outrage! A measly outrage!" shouted Shattuck. "I wish this nigger soldier and his whole varmint nation was in the middle of the Dead Sea. Just you translate that to him, will you!'

"I shall do nothing of the sort," retorted Crawford. "He is acting under orders in forbidding you to go to Damascus, and he has expressed those orders as courteously as possible. The only things you can do is to yield."

Shattuck, for answer, did the most foolish thing possible. Wheeling his horse, he endeavored to bolt past his guards.

The Turkish soldiers, representatives of the finest cavalry force in the world, had gathered about Shattuck's plunging horse before the brute had gone ten feet.

There was a short, severe scuffle, and the detective, dragged from the saddle, stood profane and writhing in the hands of his swarthy captors.

"Take him to the barracks!" ordered the officer. "Let his servant lead his horse and follow. I am desolated," he resumed, turning to the major, "that such a scene should have disturbed your evening. Good-night."

As Shattuck passed the fire under guard, May involuntarily glanced up at him. Then either the firelight or her eyes played the girl an odd trick. For she could have sworn she surprised a grin on Zenas' leathery visage. The next moment she knew she must have been mistaken, for as he caught her wondering gaze fixed on him the detective's face at once resumed its look of peevish, rebellious anger.

Taking advantage of the officer's hint, the major ordered camp broken before daybreak, and by sunrise the tourists had left the Sea of Galilee far behind them and were crossing the limestone Roman road high above the Waters of Merom.

CHAPTER VI.

ANOTHER WARNING.

By noon of the third day they passed Katana and reached the low hill overlooking Damascus.

The oldest city in the world lay stretched in the drowsy peace of countless centuries in the wide, cuplike valley below. On every side beyond its walls, orchards and quaint country-seats were scattered.

Far beyond, on the northern horizon, shimmered a broad band of yellow—the sands of the Great Syrian Desert that stretch away to distant Persia.

The myriad domes and minarets of Damascus flashed back the glittering light of the noonday sun. Through the city, like silver ribbons, ran the two scriptural rivers, Abana and Pharpar.

"This is Damascus!" the dragoman's phonograph-voice was droning. "The oldest city on earth and the most unchanged since the time of Haroun-al-Raschid.

"There are one hundred and twenty mosques in the city, including the great mosque. Damascus is built in the form of a spoon, the bowl being represented by that wide, sparsely settled tract known as the *Medan* (wide place), while the handle of the spoon is made up of the narrow streets and bazars of the more thickly populated—"

"Come," said the major, "let us get there at once."

Major Crawford, as they drew near to the huge East Gate, pointed out to the ladies the contented, "every-day" expressions and actions of the throngs of townsfolk who passed in and out.

"They don't look much like people who are planning trouble, eh?" he said triumphantly. "I never saw a busier, more contented-looking lot. And to think that people down in Jerusalem should be shaking their heads at our folly in coming!"

Smug-looking merchants, hideously deformed beggars, tall, dark Bedouins of the Desert, unwashed *fellaheen*, shrieking camel-drivers, ragged farmers from outlying districts, Jews in caps and gabardines, and with long side-locks of lank hair, haughty-looking men of splendid apparel and stately carriage—all swarmed in and out of the gateway in what would have seemed in an American city hopeless disorder and tumult, but which here in the East was merely workaday routine.

A string of camels coming out through the gateway as the tourist cavalcade was entering caused a momentary halt. May, looking with frank curiosity at the sea of swart faces and garish costumes around her, scarcely heard a word of the monologue wherewith Sir Arthur was regaling her.

"Beastly noisy, smelly place, I call it," he was saying. "It's just like a bally scene out of the 'Arabian Nights,' you know. One might almost fancy—by Jove!" he broke off at a stifled exclamation from his companion. "You look as if you were going to faint? Anything off?"

"No; I'm all right," she said slowly. "See, we can get past now. Let's hurry and catch up with the rest."

In that moment of waiting a face—upturned, eager, apprehensive—had detached itself from the throng of pedestrians about her; the face of Ralph Mohun.

As they made their way through the narrow, tortuous street toward the Hotel Basraoul, where they were to stay, May looked at the strange sights about her with eyes that saw nothing. Her brain was in a whirl.

What was Ralph Mohun doing in Damascus? Why had he come to the city, against which he had so earnestly warned her? Why, knowing their intention to come thither, had he first begged her to prevent the party from making the journey and then preceded them?

No clear reply occurred to her for any of these confused queries. But the more she conjectured, the less comprehensible did the whole matter appear.

She had noticed he was still in native dress and that his face was darkened as before by some dye.

"He wanted to get rid of us! To be sure that we should not discover him in his new hiding-place and betray him!" was the solution that at length flashed into her miserable mind.

"The coward! Oh, the *coward!* I shall never give him another thought as long as I live!"

And to prove her assertion, she spent the entire afternoon in her own room at the hotel on plea of fatigue and headache, and proceeded to cure those two ailments in true feminine fashion—by a good cry.

Dusk had fallen before May Farrar rose, bathed her throbbing eyes, and told herself for the thousandth time that Ralph Mohun was beneath her notice.

Her room on the ground floor of the rambling hotel was quite dark, but through the long, open windows the first rays of the rising moon were stealing.

She walked to the window nearest her and looked out.

The Hotel Basraoul, like nearly all caravansaries in Syria, is built about a wide courtyard. May's window, opening to the floor, gave directly on this court.

She stood looking out into the shadows of the court, where the moonlight was beginning to mark the tessellated marble pavement with strange silhouettes of fretwork. In the center of the courtyard a fountain tinkled and played. About it were flowering orange trees which filled the moonlit night with heavy fragrance.

Beyond, through an archway cut in the solid wall, May could see occasional forms pass to and fro along the street on which the hotel fronted. Somewhere near-by a woman was strumming on a native instrument and singing in the minor monotone peculiar to the East.

May Farrar stepped from her room into the stillness and fragrant beauty of the courtyard. The loveliness of the night, the fragrance of the orange flowers, the wistful cadence of the music, soothed and comforted her. She sank into a stone seat at the base of one of the orange trees and raised her hot face to the breath of the evening breeze.

"Miss Farrar!"

The voice came from the shadow of the wall just in front of her. May started to her feet. But it was not the surprise of finding she was not the sole occupant of the place nor that she should thus be addressed in English in the heart of an oriental city, that stirred her pulses and sent the blood surging in a scarlet wave to her pale face. She knew the whispered voice—would have known it at the ends of the earth. And she hated herself for the way in which the low-breathed accents stirred and thrilled her.

A man in native dress stepped from the shadow into the square of moonlight before her.

She did not need to peer into the half-concealed face to recognize Mohun.

She turned as though to go back to her room.

"Wait—just one moment!" he begged, still in the same hushed voice. "I may not get another chance to speak with you alone."

She turned on him impatiently.

"What does this mean?" she asked with imperious insistence. "Why do you dog my footsteps like this? Is it in the hope that I may humble myself before you again as I did that wretched morning when you surprised me in the Garden of Gethsemane? If so, you are destined to disappointment. A woman does not demean herself in that way the second time.

"Before you left that morning—before you ran away like a whipped cur, sneaking behind a woman's skirts for refuge—before you ran away I told you what I thought of you and how honest people regard a man of your caliber. Didn't I make it clear enough?"

"Quite."

The monosyllable, curt and impassive, checked her flood of indignation at memory of her self-abasement and his cowardice, and she found herself for the moment at a loss for words.

"Then," she began weakly enough; "then why have you forced your presence on me again?"

"To warn you—"

She interrupted him with a little, scornful laugh.

"So you said that other day. How very good of you to go about scattering mysterious warnings to all who will listen!

"Shall I tell you"—she broke off—"shall I tell you why you warned me against coming to Damascus? You intended to come here yourself to hide and you were afraid of being recognized and turned over to the police. So you tried to frighten me into dissuading my uncle from coming. Well, you failed. *Now* what warning do you want to give?"

For a second he made no reply. Then impetuously he stretched forth his hands toward her, exclaiming:

"Can't you see? Haven't you the fairness of mind to see how wrong you are? Heaven knows I've deserved no lenience at your hands, and I ask for none. But for your own sake—"

"So you said before—"

"For your own sake you *must* hear me, and you must believe me."

His vehemence held her attention—almost her belief—in spite of herself.

"You must hear me out," he repeated. "What I told you that morning of the danger of coming to Damascus was true. Then, on my way here, I heard that the military had been ordered to stop all tourists, and I felt safe about you, for I thought that even if you should be so indiscreet as to start for Damascus you would be turned back. Yet every day I have watched the East Gate in the fear of—of what I saw today."

"Well?"—as he paused.

"It is not yet too late. Go while you have time, Miss Farrar. Make some excuse—make *any* excuse—but *go.* A den of man-eating tigers would be as safe a refuge for you and yours as the city of Damascus.

"The train is laid. At any moment it may be lighted, and when it is there will be such an explosion as shall shake the civilized world to its foundations and mark this year in letters of blood and fire in the calendar of the ages. You *must* go, and go at once.

"Oh, can't you *see* I'm not lying to you, May? Can't you see I would never have followed you like this and risked your scorn and contempt if I did not—"

He paused again, checking the word he dared not speak.

"If you did not—" echoed the girl, half hypnotized by his force and pleading.

"If I did not know that you are in danger," he finished.

He was quite himself again and had his emotions well in hand.

"What is this mysterious danger you speak of?" she queried, vaguely disappointed, yet still not wholly released from the spell his words had woven.

"Massacre! The Christians and Jews of Damascus are to be slaughtered like sheep. Native and foreign alike. In the name of the prophet! The word—the signal—may be given this very night. Every day the mob that has thronged hither from all parts of Syria grows more and more restive. The leaders have difficulty in restraining the fanatics until the appointed time arrives. Daily there is some minor attack on Christians or Jews in the streets. These attacks and insults grow more violent day by day, and foreigners are especially hated. You are—"

"And believing all this, you give these poor victims no warning?"

There was a scorn mingled with incredulity in her question.

"Warning? What can I do? I have little or no knowledge of the language. I cannot warn the natives. I have gone secretly to every consulate in the city. Some consuls thought me insane; some thought I was a practical joker when I warned them of the city's fate and begged them to do something to put the Christians and Jews on their guard. Not one of them credited my story."

"Nor do I," she broke in incisively. "It is ridiculous to think that you—a foreigner—should know more than the diplomats who have lived here for years. You are either insane or—"

"You refuse to believe me?" he cried aghast.

"I certainly do. And—"

"Then," he answered with almost a groan, "there's but one thing left. If I cannot save you, I can die with you. Listen!

"I am staying at the house of Imbarak's mother in the Street of the Mehdan. It is the third house to the left before you reach the *cul-de-sac* at the end of the thoroughfare. If you need me, send there for me. The moment the massacre begins I shall be here any way at your side."

"But why," asked May, still half mockingly—for her reason told her the improbability of his story, and experience had taught her to look on him as a coward—"but why do you offer to make such a sacrifice for me?"

"Because I—" he began impetuously, but again he checked himself, stammered, and continued with a sneer of self-contempt:

"Because I am a fool, I suppose! Good-night."

His figure had melted into the shadows of the archway before May could frame a reply.

"Ralph—Mr. Mohun!" she called softly, starting forward under the sway of a sudden, irresistible impulse. But he was gone, and the echo of her own voice, vague and ghostlike, drifted back to her from the black walls of the courtyard.

CHAPTER VII.

AN EXPOSURE.

THE next few days were full of interest for the tourists, and May Farrar, heavy-hearted and abstracted as she was, forced herself to join in their countless expeditions about the quaintest, oldest and most thoroughly oriental city in the world.

To the inexperienced eyes of Major Crawford's party the populace with whom they rubbed elbows showed no signs of excitement or departure from ordinary routine. Merchant, beggar, peasant and camel-driver went about their business as usual in thorough oriental fashion.

Black looks, it is true, were occasionally cast on the group of foreigners. Here and there a guttural expletive of apparently no very complimentary nature was growled at them by some passing citizen or shrieked after them in the shrill treble of a street gamin. Knots of people collected to watch them with anything but friendly eyes and to exchange whispered comments of some sort.

But happenings such as the foregoing are the common lot of American or European tourists in an Eastern city.

Little as they knew of Syria, the major's party had long since grown accustomed to such demonstrations, and had been frequently assured in Jerusalem that the seeming hostility was merely the native form of expressing harmless disapproval of all foreigners and unbelievers.

The real signs of the times the visitors were too inexperienced to note. But it was then a mystery and remains a mystery to this day why the diplomats at the various European consulates, familiar with the Eastern temperament and forearmed as they one and all were by many and constant warnings, saw nothing alarming in the city's odd state of mind.

Daily new detachments of Bedouins, dusty from desert travel and armed to the teeth with flintlock muskets, horse-pistols and daggers, rode into the city or joined others of their brethren who were encamped directly outside the walls.

Wild-eyed fanatics—*fakirs* and dervishes alike—were traveling by hundreds along every road leading to Damascus; *fellaheen* and loafers from the mountain villages, from Lebanon to Hermon, were flocking in on all sides.

It was not the season of the year during which these various classes were wont to come to Damascus. Trade was dull, and produce was not to be bought or sold in quantities warranting such an ingress.

Moreover, the visitors, though present in such numbers that they slept by thousands in the open streets, comported themselves with a certain orderliness and quiet intensity of purpose oddly at variance with the usual behavior of the Syrian yokel when business or pleasure brings him to the metropolis.

Yet none of these things put either the proposed victims or the representatives of foreign nations on their guard. Rumors and threats of massacres are so common in that land where the only certain thing is the unexpected, that such warnings and portents as were received were treated with scorn or with apathetic indifference.

And so, lethargic as from the shock of their foreshadowed doom, the victims waited stupidly like sheep for the era of slaughter which local nobles and politicians had planned and which "the faithful" for a radius of a hundred miles had gathered to execute.

Damascus dozed under the sultry blue skies, while beneath the shadow of mosque and minaret one of the most awful tragedies in all the red annals of horror was ripening.

One morning, three days after her interview with Mohun, Miss Farrar joined the major in a walk along the Abana from the hotel to the great enclosed square used as a horse-market. The place was a babel of noise and excitement, the tramping of innumerable horses mingling with the cries of buyers, sellers and brokers.

The major, an old cavalryman, quickly caught the excitement of the scene, and wandered from group to group of the wiry, swift little horses, examining their points with the eye of a connoisseur.

May, tired of the noise, the heat and the dire confusion, said at last:

"I'll wait here under the shade of this tree while you look at the rest of the horses. Take your time. I don't mind a bit being left alone."

After the major, protesting, but secretly pleased, had departed to resume his tour of inspection, May surveyed the turbulent scene idly for a few moments, then turning back into the shade of the solitary tree she noted that the tiny patch of cool shadow was already preempted.

A man clad in the ill-fitting uniform of a Turkish gendarme stood there. He was very tall, very thin, and carried himself with a certain loose-jointed awkwardness unusual to a military man.

This oddity caused Miss Farrar to bestow a second and keener look on him, as at her approach he moved hastily away.

His face had been turned from her, but she could not mistake that shambling, slouching gait.

With a little gasp of dismay she hastened after him. The man, apparently knowing himself pursued, quickened his pace. But the passing of a consignment of horses blocked his way, forcing him to pause.

Before he could move on, May was at his side.

One look into the grizzly, leathery face, with its tight, humorous lips and shrewd light-blue eyes, sufficed the girl.

She was drawing back when Zenas Shattuck, seeing that she had recognized him, turned and faced her.

"S'prised to see *me* here, aren't ye?" he asked, grimly quizzical.

"I am indeed!" she confessed. "How did you get away from the soldiers who arrested you in Galilee, and—and *how* do you come to be wearing the uniform of a Turkish gendarme?"

"Courtesy of the police. That answers both questions. Look here, Miss Farrar, I tried to dodge you, but now that you've recognized me I know you will be telling all your friends how Zenas Shattuck's here.

"And so, while you're telling 'em, you may as well be able to tell 'em a straight story—a story that won't make me look quite like such a fool as I looked when you saw me get floored by that young scoundrel down in Jerusalem or as I looked when those heathen soldiers at the Sea of Galilee mishandled me. Care to hear about it?"

Her eager, puzzled face seemed to give him sufficient answer, for he resumed:

"Maybe it's a waste of time for me to be telling you what I'm going to do. But it riles me to have any one look on Zenas Shattuck as a jay. For I ain't one, as you'll see.

"I'll own I made a bad break when I tried to arrest that feller the very minute I got to Jerusalem instead of obeying the instructions I'd received at home and handing the native chief of police the letter I'd been given by the Turkish consul general in Boston.

"That was a mistake. But I love to play a lone hand when I can. And that time I paid pretty high for the privilege. But it was the last mistake I made. There were no others."

"Not even that night in Galilee?" May could not resist the malicious inquiry.

But Shattuck grinned as he answered:

"That doesn't come under the head of mistakes, as you'll see if you can be patient long enough to hear me out. Let's get back to the Jerusalem business first.

"Even after my man gave me the slip I still stuck to that lone-hand notion. I saw that you were the only one of your crowd who didn't raise a howl against Mr. Mohun"—pausing for a moment on the name—"and so I says to myself 'That girl'll bear watching.'

"I kept my eye on you and followed you when you went out next morning. After we came back to the hotel together I hunted up the chief of police and gave him my letter from the consul general.

"He handed me out a lot of palaver, the substance of which was that the whole Syrian police force was at my disposal, or some such flowery speech. The upshot of it was that I learned through the native police about how young Mohun had been hidden and disguised as a native by his servant, Imbarak, and how you'd fooled me into believing he was a leper when I had had my hands almost on him that morning in the Garden of Gethsemane.

"It was a slick game, and I congratulate ye on it, though it made me hot under the collar at the time."

"I don't wonder!" interpolated May, stifling a hysterical desire to laugh into the long, rueful face.

"I s'pose ye don't," he retorted calmly, "I s'pose ye don't. Well, I got further news of my man. I found he had tracked off to Damascus to get away from me.

"So I got another strong letter from the Jerusalem police chief to the chief in Damascus and I came along. I stopped overnight at the various police or military barracks on the route. That night I passed your camp I was in a hurry to get to the barracks in Tiberius.

"When the soldiers stopped me, I figured out that if I showed the officer my letters and passports, you people would know that I was coming to Damascus and you'd find a way to put Mohun on his guard.

"But if you thought I'd been turned back, you might tell him he was safe. So I raised a row and got myself taken to the barracks, where I'd been going, any way, and there I presented my letters to the right authorities. I tell you that officer who arrested me had to eat dirt by the peck.

"I was fitted out with new horses, a still stronger letter, and the uniform of a native gendarme, so that I wouldn't be picked out as an American. I got to Damascus the very morning after you did.

"I was dressed like a native, so no spies Mohun may have employed could spot me as the man who was looking for him.

"I presented my letters to the police here, and they've been scouring the place for Mohun. But they are a slow, stupid lot, and besides they seem to have something else on their minds. So I haven't nailed him yet.

"But I've got a clue at last, and I mean to have the handcuffs on his wrists before another twenty-four hours are up. I knew you and he were sweet on each other, so I've shadowed your hotel ever since I've been here, hoping he'd show up. But he hasn't.

"So I s'pose you and he are on the outs. If I'd spent less time watching *you* I could have followed up my other clue and landed him by this time."

May could hardly repress a start as she realized how nearly Mohun had been captured.

Had the detective arrived in Damascus one day earlier he must have caught the rash fugitive when the latter had sought her out in the hotel courtyard on the evening of her arrival.

"I congratulate you on your prospects," she remarked, feeling the need of saying something. "What is your clue?"

"That's telling!" Shattuck responded laconically. "How am I to know you may not be in communication with him and give the whole thing away? But," he went on, seemingly more to himself than to her, "if he hadn't been afraid to show himself he'd have hunted you up before now.

"You're the only one of your whole party who wouldn't give him up to the police on sight. I saw clear enough that the rest were all sore on him for having deceived them into making his acquaintance.

"Take my advice, miss," he added more kindly, "and forget him. He's a felon, and before another month's out he'll be behind prison bars in America, or my name's not Zenas Shattuck.'"

"Here comes my uncle," said May suddenly, her cheeks reddening under Shattuck's blunt words; "he will be interested in hearing what you've told me."

"Then he can hear it from *you!*" snapped the detective. "I ain't forgot the measly trick he tried to play me down Galilee way. And you can tell him I said so."

Shattuck slouched off into the crowd of clamorous horse-dealers just as the major came puffing up to where May stood.

"Well, my dear," exclaimed Crawford, "did I keep you waiting long? Why"—as he looked at her more closely—"you're pale. Has the heat been too much for you?"

"I'm afraid it has," she answered. "If you will take me back to the hotel I think I'll lie down for a while."

Once safe in her own room, May Farrar sat down to think out the problem that presented itself so vividly, so distressingly to her mind.

Shattuck was in Damascus, with all the powers of the local police placed at his command. Sooner or later he must surely discover Mohun.

Moreover, he had spoken of a clue that promised to lead him within twenty-four hours to his quarry's hiding-place. What could Ralph Mohun, unarmed, unprotected, with not a friend save his native groom—what could he do against the powers arrayed against him?

"He'll be arrested and carried back to America to meet the punishment he deserves!" she exclaimed, with an attempt at vindictiveness that did not deceive even herself.

"He must not! He must be saved!" her truer nature answered in the same breath. "There is no one but me to save him. No one but me to warn him that his enemy is here. What if he is a felon, as that horrid detective said? He's nothing to me. I care nothing—absolutely *nothing* for him. But he saved my life. Shall I prove less grateful than his native groom who laid *his* life in gratitude at Ralph's feet?

"Common humanity—ordinary gratitude—makes it my *duty* to warn him! If I do it to-day he can get out of Damascus before Mr. Shattuck finds him."

In this way did May Farrar work herself into the delightful belief that her interest in the fugitive was purely impersonal and that she was in duty bound to put him on his guard, much as her personal feelings shrank from the prospect of again meeting the malefactor.

But how to convey the warning?

Her first impulse was to go out at once in search of the place he had described to her: "In the Street of the Mehdan, third house to the left before you come to the *cul-de-sac* that closes the end of the street."

She knew in a general way the locality of the Street of the Mehdan, the dragoman having chanced to point it out among others on the previous day's sightseeing tour. She could find the street and follow its course to the *cul-de-sac*. And in her independent American fashion she was on the point of setting forth at once and alone.

But prudence restrained her. She knew by this time that under his unprepossessing exterior and uncouth manner Zenas Shattuck was anything but a fool.

His interview with her, like his former acts, might very readily be a ruse to put her off her guard. Knowing she had recognized him and could tell Ralph of his presence in the city, might not Zenas have pretended to be working on another clue merely to mislead her into relaxing her vigilance?

Might not he or some agent of his be even now watching the hotel in the hope that she might unconsciously lead the way to Mohun's retreat?

The thought of the indiscreet act she had meditated in going at once to Mohun now turned her sick. It was probably just the very thing Shattuck had hoped and expected she would do.

In the effort to save Mohun she would thus inadvertently have ruined him. He might even have been led to believe she had purposely guided the pursuers to his hiding-place.

And yet she *must* save him.

She considered the plan of writing him a note and sending it by one of the hotel servants. But even as the idea came to her there came with it the crushing certainty that any servant bearing a message or letter from her would infallibly be intercepted by Zenas or any police agent who might be on watch.

The long, lean detective with his awkward gait and drawling twang loomed before May's mental vision as the most powerful and baffling force she had ever encountered. But this thought brought with it its own panacea.

It aroused all the fighting instincts the girl had inherited from a long line of soldier ancestors. If the obstacle were great, then must she put forth the greater force or skill to overcome it.

If Shattuck were subtle she would match her woman's wit against his and win! The idea thrilled and braced her.

"I have it!" she cried at last, springing to her feet.

Her resolution taken, she lost no time in putting it into effect.

CHAPTER VIII.

TO THE RESCUE.

THE plan May Farrar had evolved was based on Shattuck's observation that she alone of all the party had refrained from speaking ill of Ralph. The detective regarded the others as Mohun's enemies.

If she should go for an apparently aimless stroll with one of her traveling companions, the detective would certainly not imagine she was bound for Mohun's retreat

Her mind rapidly ran over the list.

Her uncle? He would never consent to be a party to such a scheme and would veto it from the start.

Mrs. Sharpe? The little old lady's kindly heart might induce her to become an accomplice, but she was so timid she would never stir abroad in the streets without masculine escort.

Sir Arthur Cole? At first May scoffed at this last notion, but in an inspiration she saw that he and he alone was the man for her purpose. The young Englishman's cheerful stupidity, his blind and blatant infatuation for herself, would make him an ideal assistant in such an enterprise.

Her conscience smote her at thought of thus taking advantage of the young Englishman's fatuous adoration, but it seemed the only way whereby Ralph could be helped.

Ten minutes later she entered the reading-room of the hotel, dressed for walking and drawing on her gloves. Sir Arthur Cole sat sprawled upon a wicker lounging chair, puffing at a cigarette and yawning in a dreary, bored fashion.

At sight of the girl in her dainty walking-suit, fluffy parasol, and wide picture hat, Cole scrambled to his feet, threw away his cigarette and came forward, the bored look merging into a grin of welcome.

"By Jove, you do look fit!" he declared. "Whither away? For more sightseeing? "

"No. Just for a walk and for an errand," she replied.

"Might I come, too?" he asked, eagerly grabbing up his sun-helmet and walking-stick from the window-seat.

May appeared to weigh his request doubtfully.

"If you'll promise not to ask questions as to where I'm going," she decided at last, with a purposed affectation of wilful command; "and if you'll promise to do just as I say and if you'll promise not to tell any one where we've been. There! Can you make all three pledges?"

The young man, suspecting vaguely that he was being chaffed, but not seeing the point of the joke, answered readily:

"I promise all three. Now let's be off. Luncheon is in an hour, and I hate to miss my meals. Don't you?"

Together they set out, talking gaily and sauntering along as if they had no especial destination. Cole was in the seventh heaven of conceited delight at the unusual friendliness his companion exhibited and the kind way in which she laughed at his labored witticisms.

May saw no one in the vicinity of the hotel whom she could identify as a spy.

A ragged Arab beggar lay asleep in the sun, across the road. A Bedouin, fierce of eye, swarthy of skin, stalked haughtily down the middle of the thoroughfare, gun on back.

Stray scavenger dogs snapped and snarled at each other in the dust. But for these the suburban district was deserted.

"I'm going to see an old woman in the native quarter," May vouchsafed as they crossed the Abana and reached the more densely populated part of town.

Then she added to herself in self-justification: "Ralph said himself that he was stopping at the house of Imbarak's mother. So I really *am* going to see an old woman—if she's at home."

"What a bore!" ejaculated Cole. "Old women are so stupid."

"Then you shall stay outside while I pay my visit," decreed Miss Farrar. "I won't have you yawning and looking at your watch and fidgeting me all the time I'm there. You shall stay in the road outside and you shan't have even a glimpse at the old woman."

"But—" began Cole, puzzled yet relieved.

"You promised to obey," she reminded him.

Had she been less absorbed, and had he been less thick of head, neither could well have failed to notice the electrically charged atmosphere that seemed to pervade the crowd who packed the narrow, winding streets.

There was a change, an important and visible change, in the demeanor of the townsfolk since the preceding day. Every one seemed to be waiting for something; to be keyed to highest tension; to anticipate nervously yet eagerly some great event.

The black looks and muttered maledictions that usually followed in the wake of the foreigners were to-day more overt than ever before, and it was with relief that May turned into the less-frequented Street of the Mehdan.

The little thoroughfare opened off the public square at the back of the farther bazars and was barely a thousand feet in length. Before her May could descry a high stone wall shutting off the end of the shallow, wide street and forming a *cul-de-sac*.

She began counting the houses, at length singling out one which stood in a walled garden, the door being let into the outer street-wall.

"Stop here!" she commanded Sir Arthur, "here in the shade and wait for me. Smoke all the cigarettes you can in the interval, for I shall only be in the house for a few moments."

Gathering up her waning courage, May advanced to the door in the wall and rapped.

A little iron grille was slid back almost at once, and the girl felt herself the cynosure of an unseen pair of eyes. She heard the person on the other side of the wall withdraw, and shuffling, slippered footsteps crossing the narrow court which separated the wall from the house itself.

Then the sound of murmured voices talking in Arabic reached her, and afterward a slightly louder voice which she quickly recognized as Imbarak's, speaking in English as though interpreting. A faster footfall crossed the little flagged court, the grille was again slipped back, and she knew she was once more under scrutiny.

Then the heavy, iron-banded door slowly swung part way open, and Imbarak, standing where he could not be seen by any one else in the street, beckoned her to enter.

Annoyed by these excessive precautions and the double surveillance, May Farrar stepped boldly into the yard. As she did so the gate clanged shut behind her, and Imbarak lowered the great steel bar that served as a bolt.

Having thus secured the entrance, the groom salaamed low before the visitor.

"The *howaji* is within," he was beginning, when Ralph Mohun himself, still in native dress, brushed past a sweet-faced, elderly woman whose portly form filled the narrow doorway of the house.

"Miss Farrar!" he exclaimed. "I could hardly believe Imbarak when he told me it was you at the outer gate. May I present you to my hostess, Imbarak's mother? She has been most kind to me. I owe her and her son everything. I—"

But May, acknowledging the introduction and the old lady's reverential salute by a formal and brief bow, interrupted Mohun by saying:

"I can stay but a moment. May speak with you alone?"

Imbarak and his mother withdrew to the interior of the house before the girl could regret her bruskness of manner or note the slight look of pain that crossed Ralph's stained face at this summary dismissal of his hosts.

"May I suggest, Miss Farrar," he began stiffly, "that whatever contempt I may have merited at your hands, this woman and her son deserve all courtesy. Pardon my mentioning it, but they have done everything for me, and I regret that you saw fit to show them so little consideration."

May felt that the rebuke was merited, and already her naturally kindly nature was reproaching her for her thoughtless words and curt manner. But it irked her that the reproof should come from a man whom she was befriending at so much risk.

"I might have expected some such greeting," she retorted bitterly, "but luckily I came here merely to perform an act of human kindness, and not in the hope of any especial civility from you. Let me state my business, and go. Mr. Zenas Shattuck, the detective who tried to arrest you in Jerusalem, is here in Damascus, and boasts that he will capture you within twenty-four hours."

"In Damascus!" echoed Mohun in dismay. "You must be mistaken."

"I have talked with him this morning. He is dressed as a gendarme, and he has the assistance of the whole Damascus police force. I came to warn you. To prove"—she laughed in an embarrassed fashion—"to prove that you don't hold a monopoly on warnings. Save yourself while you can!"

He was looking at her with an expression she had never before seen in his dark eyes. It disconcerted her and set her heart to beating in a rapid, tumultuous way that angered her.

"And *you* bring me word? You do this for *me?*" he murmured at last.

"Not for *you,* but out of ordinary gratitude for what you did for me at the Jordan. And now I must go. Oh, *why* did you ever—" She was about to add "cross my path?" but checked the inexplicable, sudden impulse that rose within her and changed the words to "Why did you ever come here?"

"Why did I come? Because I knew the authorities would try to avoid complications with foreign powers by forbidding foreigners to enter Damascus while the massacre was pending. Because I thought I should be safe from pursuit here. How your party and Shattuck eluded the soldiers, who had orders to turn back all tourists, I don't know. I thought that here I should be safe until—"

"Safe in the storm-center of a massacre?" she interrupted incredulously. "If your warnings to me had been true, if there were really any danger of a massacre, this would scarcely seem to be a safe place for you."

"It was capture, not death, that I feared," he answered. "I can't explain. And it doesn't matter in any case—except to me."

"No," she assented slowly, "you *can't* explain. That is very clear. It is one of *many* things you can't or won't explain. And yet"—her voice trembled ever so little—"I'd have given *everything* to be able to believe in you."

Again that strange light in his eyes, as he took an instinctive step toward her swayed the girl's heart with new and wonderful, yet unwelcome, emotions.

"Good-by!" she said briefly. "Leave Damascus to-day. To-morrow may be too late. And if it is any comfort to you to know it, a foolish girl will always pray for your safety."

She had not meant to say it. The words had forced themselves from her unwilling lips. She colored and turned toward the gate.

"God bless and keep you always!" muttered the man brokenly.

A mist of tears blinded her for the instant as she stepped into the glaring noonday light of the street. But she was aware of noise, jeering, and laughter directly ahead of her.

Her eyes accustoming themselves to the glare, she saw Sir Arthur Cole surrounded by half a hundred men and boys who had been drawn by the unusual sight of a foreigner in that obscure quarter, and who were subjecting the stolid Englishman to every form of insult and gibe that the malicious oriental mind could devise.

Seeing the girl, they drew back in momentary surprise. Then one practical joker in the throng shoved another man forward.

The latter jostled Cole roughly. The Englishman, losing control of himself at this ignominy, lifted his stout walking-stick and belabored his assailant over the head.

In an instant the laughter and jesting had changed into an ominous growl. Knives flashed, and the crowd moved forward as one man.

Cole backed to the wall beside which May stood trembling, and raised his stick in futile defense. Then at sight of the ring of dark, vengeful faces and the glitter of the short, crooked knives a wave of panic fear encompassed him.

Forgetful of the frightened girl, of the precepts of manhood, of everything save his own mortal danger, Cole dropped his stick; leaped up and caught the bough of a tree that projected over the wall from a neighboring garden, and by a frantic effort swung himself to the top of the wall and over on the opposite side just in time to miss a knife-lunge.

The baffled natives gibbered and swore. Suddenly one of them, pointing to the forsaken girl, yelled in exultation to his fellows:

"The *feringhee* has gone, but the *feringhee sit* remains. That is vengeance enough!"

With a howl of fanatical hatred the mob rushed upon May, who shrank cowering against the wall, covering her white face with her hands.

CHAPTER IX.

"YOU ARE THE MAN I CALLED A COWARD."

THE spark of race enmity and religious hatred that had smoldered in Damascus burst into blaze when Sir Arthur Cole struck down his chief tormentor at the moment of May Farrar's reappearance in the Street of the Mehdan.

You can kick an Egyptian and he will cringe. You can kick a Hindoo and he will lick your boots. But molest a Syrian and his knife will be between your ribs, before you have time to argue out the supreme rights of the Anglo-Saxon.

England in her Sepoy mutiny and later in the Alexandria massacre of 1882 learned to her cost that even an oft-kicked Hindoo and Egyptian will at length exact usurious payment for every seemingly unresented kick. The Syrian does not leave the debt so long unpaid.

The men and boys who had gathered about Cole as he stood in the empty street had probably had no definite object beyond baiting and annoying one of the detested *Inglese*. But the ill-advised blow of his walking-stick had in one instant turned the rude sport into murderous attack.

The fanatical hatred against the Christian and foreigner which had been so thoroughly instilled in their hearts, and which many of them had been summoned to Damascus to gratify, flamed up at the blow. A braver man than Cole might have been pardoned for fleeing before that grim face of death so suddenly flashed in his eyes. To do the Englishman justice, his bewilderment, rage and subsequent panic had been so great that he had not realized May's return from the house, nor had he noticed her, although she had stood closely by his side.

Baffled by their victim's sudden escape, the mob, now greatly augmented in numbers, readily turned its fury against the American girl.

With a roar from a hundred throats they were upon her where she crouched trembling against the wall, her hands pressed convulsively over her eyes to shut out the sea of mad faces that surged and billowed about her. The foremost of the assailants, a gigantic Bedouin from east of the Jordan, had already gripped her shoulder. The shock of the rude contact wrung a scream of terror from her numbed lips.

"Ralph!" she shrieked, not realizing what words she found to voice her terror. "Ralph! Help me!"

The hot breath of the jostling front rank of assassins was in her face. The Bedouin's grip was dragging her from the shelter of the wall. The whole scene since Cole's escape had not occupied five seconds.

Before the first cry had fairly left her lips, a crashing, roaring sound close to her ear well-nigh deafened her. She felt the Bedouin's hold relax, and, glancing up, saw him spin about like an automaton and collapse in a heap in the dust of the unpaved roadway.

Again the deafening sound rang out and this time she realized it was a pistol shot.

Another man who, knife raised, had pressed close behind the Bedouin, screamed, *"Allah! Il Allah!"* and tumbled writhing to the ground. The rest of the mob involuntarily gave back a step, and as they did so May Farrar felt herself swung lightly from the ground.

Strong arms grasped her closely, and she knew that the man who had lifted her was running.

She had not time to catch her breath before she was carried through a low gateway and a door was slammed and barred behind her.

As she was gently set upon her feet, a wild shriek of rage from without proved that the mob had recovered from its momentary pause of amazement and had rallied to the attack.

Raising her eyes, she saw Ralph Mohun, a long navy revolver still clenched in his right hand, looking down at her with frightened solicitude, while just beyond Imbarak was strengthening the fastenings of the gate against which the crowd was already pounding.

"Are you hurt?" asked Ralph, still panting slightly from his strenuous exertion.

She looked at him for a full minute without a reply, while the crowd outside hammered in vain at the stout portal, filling the sultry mid-day air with hideous clamor.

Slowly she realized that, drawn by her cry, Mohun had leaped out among her enemies, had silenced forever two of them, had caught her up and had carried her to safety at the risk of being torn to pieces by the pack of assassins.

His native dress, the audacity of the sortie, and their amaze that a man apparently of their own number should thus turn on them accounted for the natives' brief pause of dismay to which the American man and girl owed their lives.

"Tell me," repeated Mohun entreatingly, raising his voice to be heard above the outside turmoil, "are you hurt? For God's sake, speak! If they have harmed one hair of your head—"

She opened her lips and he checked his agonized words to listen.

"And you," she said dully, "and *you* are the man I called a *coward!*"

She glanced shamefacedly toward Imbarak and his mother, who stood in silence beside the gate, then, walking across to the sweet-faced old Syrian lady, May held out her hand.

"I want you, please, to forgive my rudeness when I was here before," began the girl bravely; "I was hardly myself. I—I—Oh, I am *very* much ashamed."

Somehow, in inexplicable feminine fashion, the two women—oriental and occidental—suddenly found themselves crying in each other's arms. Mohun discreetly turned his back and joined Imbarak in examining the gate fastenings.

But neither woman noticed him.

When the tears and the embrace were over, May and the old lady were fast friends, and the girl was carried off by her hostess into the interior of the house for a cup of coffee.

So self-centered had the occupants of the courtyard been, and so common are street rows in Syrian cities, that it was only now that Imbarak noted the cessation of the tumult outside the gate. He went to the little iron grille and pushed aside the shutter.

"Have they gone, Imbarak?" queried Mohun.

"No, sir. I can't quite understand. The street is now packed from end to end. Most of the people seem gathered about something on the ground, Oh! Now a man has jumped on a rubbish heap and is addressing them. He is the *imam* (priest) of the Mehdan mosque. Wait! I can hear his words!"

Little as he knew of the East, Imbarak's words brought a deep meaning to Mohun. He saw that the crowd, its momentary blind fury past, had taken fuller cognizance of the two men he had shot, and that they had stopped to consult as to the step which this grave phase of the situation might entail.

A shout, no longer a mere yell of rage, but fraught with a deeper, deadlier note, rose from the packed masses in the shallow wide street as sentence after sentence of the *imam's* sonorous harangue sank into their minds.

"What does he say, Imbarak?" asked Ralph.

"It is bad news, *howaji*," responded the groom, turning from the grille. "He is a great man in this neighborhood and his words carry weight. He is a chief mover in the massacre.

"He says an inmate of my house has slain Sheik Ali Diab of the El Kaneh tribe of Bedouins, and has also mortally wounded Halil Raad, a respected merchant of the Skuri quarter, and that the aforesaid inmate did this in preventing the people of Damascus from rightly putting to death a *feringhee* sorceress.

"The murderer, he says, was dressed as a Mohammedan and is doubtless a renegade and spy. He says you and the *sit* must be given up to the people for death. Wait, sir!" he ended, as a heavy knock sounded at the gate.

"Imbarak Abou-Najib!" called a loud voice.

The groom returned to the grille and a brief parley ensued between himself and a man outside.

"There will be trouble, *howaji*—much trouble," he reported after he had again closed the grating. "The *imam* formally demanded that I give you and the *sit* to the crowd for death. If I would do so at once, he said, I and my mother should be pardoned for having harbored you both. Otherwise—"

"Otherwise?"

"Otherwise he says the people will storm my home and kill us all with tortures."

"And you replied?"

"Howaji!" cried Imbarak, his voice fraught with hurt dignity as he drew himself to his full height, "there could be but one reply for me to make. You saved my life. You and the *sit* have broken bread with us. Your safety is our safety. Your death is my death. Allah be my witness!"

"But, Imbarak," protested Mohun, "you must not do this for me. I cannot allow it. When you offered to help me to escape to Damascus and to give me shelter in your mother's house here, I accepted the offer and insisted on paying you—so far as money could pay for such service.

"But this is a different thing. You cannot risk your life and your mother's life for me. I'm not cur enough to permit that."

"Where are you going, *howaji?*" asked the groom as Mohun strode toward the gate.

"I am going out to sell my life to those murderers at as high a price as the contents of my two revolvers will bring," replied Ralph, as he lifted the great steel bar of the gate.

"And the *sit?*"

The bar clanged back in place. Mohun stood irresolute.

"If you go," resumed Imbarak, quick to follow his advantage, "you will only deprive Miss Farrar of one defender and will not make matters any better. For the crowd demands her life as well as yours. And you surely cannot mean to give her up to their mercy!"

"What am I to do?" murmured Ralph in dire perplexity. "If I give myself up to them, can't you help Miss Farrar to escape by some rear way?"

"It is too late, *howaji*. The house and garden are surrounded by this time. And even if there were a safe exit for her, could you not also take advantage of it? No, howaji, there is but one thing for us all to do. We must stay here and fight it out together as long as we can hold the house against them. The police will soon arrive and rescue us.

"Till then, every man counts. Your place is here. You have your revolvers, I have my father's fowling-piece and the Winchester rifle we bought last week in the bazaars.

"There is much ammunition, though little food," he added under his breath. "Listen! The *imam* has told them my decision. In another minute they will attack.

"They are doubtless waiting until a log or beam can be fetched from one of the bazaars to serve as a battering-ram against the gate or until a ladder can be brought from the nearest orchard for scaling the wall.

"That's why they aren't making more noise. If they were just out for a row, they would all be screaming like wildcats, but they mean death; that is why they wait in patience."

He stopped abruptly as a rustling sound from the house door behind apprized him for the first time that his mother and May Farrar had returned from the inner rooms in time to overhear the last part of the conversation.

"Mr. Mohun," said May quietly yet intently, "do I understand that our presence here means danger to our hosts?"

"The gravest danger," assented Ralph, "and—"

"Then"—as calmly as if taking her leave at an afternoon tea—"shall we go?"

"You must not!" cried Imbarak. "I have explained that to the *howaji*. And even if you should give yourselves up," he continued mendaciously, "it is now too late to save my mother and myself from the fury of your enemies. For I was offered my choice and I refused with insults to surrender you. So I, too, am marked for slaughter. We must all stand together in this."

The lull in the crowd's clamor had ceased while the groom was speaking, and the walled street now reëchoed with clash of arms and jargon of dissonant voices.

"The battering-ram or the ladder must have arrived," conjectured Ralph.

"No," contradicted Imbarak, more used to the various phases of Eastern mobs and able to catch and translate a stray phrase here and there in the bellowed jangle of guttural Arabic. "No. There is a new diversion of some kind. What can it be?"

As though in direct response to the groom's query, a rasping, drawling voice, cutting like a knife through the volume of looser sounds, came to the ears of the besieged.

The speaker stood just without the gate, having evidently fought his way thither by main force.

"I don't speak your blamed heathen lingo," the high-pitched tones began, "and I don't want to. But maybe some of you can understand good English and translate it to the rest. I'm not trying to interfere with your sport, whatever that form of diversion may be, and I don't want any of you interfering with *me* in the discharge of my duty.

"I am an officer of the Boston detective force, and I'm here to arrest a criminal who has taken refuge in this house. And I'm going to have him if I have to lick the whole crowd of you. Your Damascus police traced him here to-day, and I'm going to nab him without waiting for any departmental red tape."

Ralph had started violently at the first sound of Zenas Shattuck's voice.

Now he moved forward to the grille, slid aside the shutter, and peeped through the slits of the iron grating.

Shattuck, still clad as a Turkish gendarme, stood with his back to the gate. About him clustered the close-packed native mob.

The spectacle of a Turkish policeman had for the moment stopped them. The further surprise of hearing this man address them in a language and tone utterly foreign to the Orient had still further amazed them. But now one man farther back in the crowd cut short the Bostonian's speech with a yell of anger.

"He is *Inglese!* A *feringhee!*" bawled the native. "He says so himself. He has stolen the uniform of a believer and masquerades before us to make mock of our laws. By the beard of my father—"

He said no more. His words, caught up and repeated in a thousand varying shades of fanatical frenzy, drowned further attempt to speak.

The mob surged forward. Shattuck was dashed against the gate with a force that made the stout, iron-bound timbers creak.

The staff of a countryman resounded on the detective's unprotected head before the nearest knife thrust could reach him.

Zenas fell like one dead across the threshold of the gate, and fifty knives gleamed over his defenseless, inert body.

Imbarak, in the narrow courtyard where the four fugitives were huddled, sprang forward, but too late to avert an action of Mohun's which the groom had just foreseen.

The bar was thrown upward by one wrench of Ralph's strong arm, and the gate was swung quickly open.

The assassins saw the glint of a revolver barrel, and three shots in lightning succession were fired into the jammed mass of besiegers.

Before a blow could be struck in reprisal, Ralph had stooped, seized the unconscious detective by the collar, dragged him inside the courtyard, and shut the gate.

Imbarak hurled the steel bar into place by the time the gate was fairly closed.

CHAPTER X.

A FIGHT FOR LIFE.

A YELL, compared to which all former efforts on the part of the crowd were as mere whispers, burst from the baffled mob. Zenas Shattuck lay stretched along the narrow pavement of the courtyard, and the man to whose presence of mind and swift audacity he owed his life stood above him coolly reloading his revolver.

"Ralph!" gasped May Farrar.

He turned to look at her. She leaned, dead white and fainting, against the lintel of the house door, her horror-stricken eyes fixed on Mohun.

"Yes?" he said inquiringly, stepping toward her, while Imbarak and his mother worked over the unconscious Shattuck.

"How insane! How foolhardy of you!" she panted. "It was all so quick, all so sudden, I couldn't realize it until it was all over. You might have been killed!"

"The chances *were* in favor of it," he admitted, "but a sortie was the very last thing they were expecting out there, and so I reckoned on the element of surprise to get me through it safely."

He spoke with intentional matter-of-fact carelessness, but she was not to be turned from the trend of thought into which his act had plunged her.

"It was heroic!" she declared. "Why make light of it? But it was the most quixotic, insane thing a man ever did. If you had left him to the mob you would have been safe from him forever. His death meant your freedom. You never thought of that?"

"There wasn't overmuch time for thought," he answered; "yet it happens I did think of it. One thinks quickly when one has to. I weighed all it might mean, pro and con, to me, even while I was lifting the bar of the gate."

"And yet you did it!"

"Why," he replied in perplexity, "what else was there for me to do? They would have murdered him in another second. He had to be rescued."

"He is your enemy."

"He is an American. I'm not a man to make the eagle scream on all occasions, as perhaps you know. Nor do I use the Stars and Stripes to signal omnibuses with. But, after all, we're Americans together, Shattuck and I, in a foreign and hostile land, and if I'd stood by and let a lot of beggarly orientals murder him, I could never have dared lift my hat to the dear old flag again. I'm sorry, though, if I caused you any shock or fright. Shall I get you a glass of *mastik?*"

"No," she said, ashamed of her show of emotion; "I'm all right now. Can't we do anything to help Mr. Shattuck?"

They crossed to where Imbarak crouched with the detective's head on his knee, while his mother bathed the wound in Shattuck's scalp and chafed his temples with *mastik.*

Zenas' lean, leathery face and grizzled hair were caked with blood and dust. His uniform was in rags and half-torn from his back.

The blow that had felled him had been supplemented by sundry kicks. Ralph had been right in saying that in one second more the mob would have killed the detective outright.

Slowly Shattuck's shrewd light-blue eyes opened. He stared wildly about him. Then his vague glare narrowed and concentrated as it fell on Mohun.

"You're my prisoner!" he croaked harshly, and sank back into unconsciousness.

Mohun and Imbarak carried the limp body into the house and laid it on a mattress. As they returned, leaving the groom's mother to tend the sick man, a cheer from without the gates sent Imbarak running to the grille.

"They've got it!" he exclaimed.

"Battering-ram or ladder?" queried Ralph.

"Ladder!" was the laconic response. "Two of them," he added an instant later.

Imbarak rushed into the house and returned, staggering under the weight of a huge muzzle-loading fowling-piece, a Winchester rifle, a big Colt's revolver of ancient design, and a basket containing ammunition. A rusty saber dangled by a cord from his wrist.

"Don't bring those out here," directed Ralph, who, pistol in hand, was watching their enemies through the grille. "The mob may rush this courtyard. Leave the arms in the passageway where we can get them, and where they will be safe in case we have to retreat into the house in a hurry. What on earth are the local police and soldiery thinking of to let a crowd like that collect out there?"

"The police are our one hope, *howaji*," returned Imbarak, ramming a heavy charge of powder into the fowling-piece and measuring out some slugs in the palm of his hand. "It is against the interests of the nobles and the politicians to allow any uprising or riot before the moment that everything is ripe and the signal is given for the massacre.

"Even those nearest the leaders do not know when that signal is to be given, though every one has hourly awaited it for weeks. As soon as the police learn there is a disturbance here in the Street of the Mehdan a squadron of cavalry will scatter the rioters!"

"And how about us?"

"We will be taken to the *serail* (palace of justice) and examined. We will doubtless be released, as we have acted in self-defense. Our one hope now is to hold off the crowd, killing as few as possible, until the military arrive. It cannot be long now—"

Even as he spoke they heard the impact of a ladder placed on the opposite side of the wall and saw its rungs rising above the ten-foot barrier.

"Shall I shoot the first head?" asked Ralph.

"No; I have a better plan. Let us throw the ladder back. Together we should be strong enough."

Both sprang to the top of the wide, five-foot ledge that runs along the inside of most Damascus walls, and scarcely had they gained it when the first head appeared over the wall.

Smash went Mohun's fist into the center of the climber's ferocious visage. The head vanished and they heard a yell as the man fell back among his fellows. But others were on the ladder, and the top of a fez appeared over the edge.

Mohun and the groom had grasped the tip of the ladder by this time, and at a concerted effort sent it, with its load of climbers, toppling back into the crowd.

The same instant the roaring report of a horse-pistol sounded, and Mohun's fez leaped from his head. Glancing to the right, the defenders saw that, unnoticed, the second ladder had been reared into place several yards farther on.

The foremost scaler had already swung himself to the top of the wall, had discharged one of his horse-pistols at Ralph, and was now in the act of leaping down into the yard. A second man was scrambling from the ladder top to the summit of the wall, and the head of a third appeared immediately behind.

Ralph whipped out his own revolver and fired point blank at the native who had already gained a footing in the courtyard. The shot seemed very easy, yet, like many easy shots, it missed.

The fellow had meantime drawn his second horse-pistol, and was covering Ralph, while the second man on the wall had reached down for something on the outer side and now regained his equilibrium, brandishing a bell-mouthed blunderbuss.

Imbarak was behind Mohun on the ledge, and seeing the latter's imminent peril he leaped from the ledge into the courtyard just as the man with the horse-pistol drew trigger.

The sudden advent of Imbarak at his very feet disconcerted his aim and the ball whizzed harmlessly past Ralph's ear. A third man, a dervish, wild-eyed and grotesque of garb, had gained the top of the wall behind the man with the blunderbuss.

As Ralph was taking aim at the latter, the dervish, with dagger raised and calling shrilly on Allah, sprang along the summit like a cat.

The man with the blunderbuss had his weapon at his shoulder. A bare dozen yards separated him from Mohun.

Knowing that such weapons often contain several ounces of lead, scrap-iron and other heterogeneous projectiles, and that their destructive power at short range is almost equal to that of a gatling gun, Ralph at once made his choice between the marksman and the nearer dervish.

His navy revolver spoke. The man with the blunderbuss bounced off the wall in grotesque fashion as though shot from a catapult.

The dervish at one bound was upon Ralph. Mohun had not time to fire again nor even to raise his weapon. The long-curved knife blazed before his eyes.

The dervish's yell was in his ears, and the glaring eyeballs, the distorted brown face and the writhing body were carved forever upon the helpless American's memory.

Then the dervish dropped his knife, clapped both hands to his own shoulder, staggered, lost his footing, and whirled to the ground, his fantastic robes billowing and flapping as he fell. It had all happened in the twinkling of an eye. Ralph had not so much as had time to raise and cock his revolver when his foe thus mysteriously vanished.

He glanced downward into the courtyard. Imbarak and the first invader were locked in a death-grip, swaying back and forth in the narrow, walled space.

Help had evidently not come from that quarter. But just behind the wrestlers was May Farrar. Her hand grasped a small revolver from which a tiny stream of smoke was still curling.

Ralph remembered the weapon. It was one which Major Crawford had given May on the day they had landed in Palestine, and the major had instructed her never to stir abroad without it. Ralph's gaze passed from the pistol to the girl's face.

Their eyes met in the briefest of glances, then Mohun turned again to the grim work in hand.

The wall was for the instant clear, the wholesale repulse having temporarily dampened the zeal of the besiegers. But the first ladder was once more being set into place, and the trembling of the upper rungs nearest him told Ralph that a second assault was preparing.

The two ladders were fully fifty feet apart. Ralph could not hope to be at both vantage points at once. He sprang to the ground and took up his position in the doorway of the house, both revolvers drawn.

"My only hope is to keep the top of the wall clear by shooting," he explained hastily to May as he passed her.

"Go into the house at once," he added peremptorily; "this is no place for you."

"It was the place for me a moment ago," she retorted. "I shall stay here and do my share."

"You will do as I say and go indoors at once!" he commanded. No man had ever used such a tone toward her before and to her bewilderment she not only found herself meekly obeying the order but experiencing a strange sense of joy in being thus mastered.

Imbarak still struggled with the burly giant whom he had grappled. Mohun dared not shoot at the intruder for fear of hurting the groom, and he could not leave his post of duty to descend into the courtyard for the purpose of aiding Imbarak. So, watching the two ladder tops keenly, he yet kept a sidelong surveillance of the straggling pair in the courtyard, ready, the instant they should momentarily separate, to fire the conclusive shot.

"Oh, where are the police?" he groaned to himself. "Surely they should be here by now. I can't hold the courtyard against another rush without Imbarak's help. And what are those vermin out there waiting for?"

For no heads had appeared above the wall. The besiegers seemed waiting for something, and the suspense told more sharply on Ralph Mohun's nerves than had the heat of battle.

But he was not to be left long in doubt as to the nature of the surprise his opponents were meditating, nor as to the cause of their unaccountable delay.

CHAPTER XI.

THE DISTANT BELL.

EVEN as Ralph Mohun, pistol in hand, stood alert in the doorway watching the upper rungs of the two ladders protruding over the top of the wall in front of him, the ends of a third ladder and then of a fourth appeared. The besiegers, realizing the peril and the waste of time involved in seeking to storm the place with only two ladders, had secured more.

They knew the puny numerical strength of the defenders and counted wisely on the certainty that two men could not repel a concerted rush from four separate points.

At the moment the fourth ladder appeared, Imbarak, in the courtyard, tripped and threw his heavy assailant. The falling man's head struck a sharp angle of the wall and he lay stunned from the impact.

By the time his foe's body had touched the ground Imbarak's short, curved knife was drawn. But Mohun's warning shout dissuaded him from his purpose.

Following the direction of Ralph's eyes, he noted the augmented number of ladders and was quick to realize the significance.

"In! In and barricade the doors!" he cried, gaining the doorway just as the foremost head appeared over the wall.

A Bedouin, gaining the summit, fired his long gun at the pair as they closed the house door, the charge of buckshot striking harmlessly against the massive iron-studded panels.

After the glare of the outer court the two men could at first scarcely accustom their eyes to the cool gloom of the interior, but they groped their way about, closing and barring shutters and piling heavy barriers against the front and rear doors.

The house of Imbarak's mother, like hundreds of other residences in that city, had been built in the days when a Damascene's home was his castle.

It was guarded in front, as has been seen, by a ten-foot wall separated by a narrow courtyard from the house itself. Adjoining buildings formed a line continuous with the front of the house.

At the rear, however, was the usual neglected rose-garden in whose center played a tiny fountain whence the family's supply of drinking-water was derived.

The high sides of surrounding houses walled in this garden, the only means of ingress being the rear door of the residence itself.

In common with nearly every Damascene dwelling, heavy iron bars protected the lower windows, front and back, and these were further reinforced by iron shutters, each provided with the usual tiny, crescent-shaped loophole.

Of the five rooms within, four were on the ground floor. A very narrow stone staircase led to the second story, whose entire space was occupied by a wide, low-ceiled room or loft. From this half a dozen steps in one corner communicated with the roof. The roofs, in Damascus, as in all Eastern cities, are flat, guarded on all sides by three-foot parapets of stone, and serve as sitting-room, bedroom, chapel and general "living-place" for the entire family.

Having made all secure down-stairs, Mohun and Imbarak repaired to the loft, barricaded its solitary window, and then proceeded to batten down the trap leading to the roof.

With a glance of satisfaction Imbarak glanced about at the completed preparations.

"Decidedly," he said, "our ancestors who built these houses knew what they were about. This building is of stone and stucco, therefore it cannot be burned from without. The windows are barred, and the doors are so strong that it would take an hour to beat them down even with a battering-ram, and long before an hour is up the police and soldiery are sure to hear of the disturbance, even in this obscure district of the city, and to disperse the crowd."

The besiegers had filled the courtyard and were thundering at the front door, striving with axes, clubs and even with knives to batter down the ironbound portal.

"But surely the police must have got wind of the thing before this?" hazarded May. "The noise alone could be heard half a mile, I should think."

"They'll be here at any moment now," said Mohun, "and you will be safe at your hotel in another hour."

"But *you?*" she asked.

"I—I shall not be taken," he replied in a low voice.

"But what can you do?"

"Resist arrest. That will settle matters very quickly."

"You mustn't! How can you think of such a thing?"

"If I am captured I shall be sent back to America a prisoner."

"And you actually prefer—?"

"I prefer anything to that. Death is not hard to bear if one face it like a man, but—there are reasons why I must not return to America. I cannot explain them to you."

"But after all you have done for me—"

"Miss Farrar," he interposed with a touch of his former stiffness of manner, "my future cannot in any way concern or interest you. You have not hesitated to tell me so yourself more than once. Shan't we drop the subject?"

Imbarak, who had been to look at Shattuck, now reëntered the room.

"It is lucky the police are sure to raise the siege so soon," he observed, "for we have scarcely a day's provisions in the house and barely a half-pint of water. Mr. Shattuck is delirious and clamoring for it, but we have so little I refused it to him. It is best to save it for some one worthier than that human bloodhound."

"But there is a fountain in the garden behind the house," suggested May. "I saw it when I came in."

For answer, Imbarak signed to her to come to the rear window. Through the crescent peep-hole she could command a view of the three houses whose sides formed the walls of the garden. On the roofs of all three sat armed men.

"They are waiting for a chance to shoot," said Imbarak in explanation. "They know we have a wounded man here. They know the day is hot and he will need water. They hope some of us may venture out to the fountain.

"Yes," he continued, speaking loudly to be heard above the din at the door, "it is lucky our siege here is to be so brief. If it were to last longer—"

He broke off with a gasp of dismay.

"What's the matter?" asked Mohun.

But Imbarak raised his hand for silence and seemed listening intently. And in the momentary hush that followed they all heard what his keener ear had at once detected—the tolling of a distant bell.

The besiegers, too, had evidently heard the sound, for a stillness as of death fell on them. And through the silence, again and again, louder and more insistent, came the solely booming notes of the great bell.

"Allah sa-id! (God help us!)" gasped Imbarak.

And on the instant there rose from the entire city a mighty sound of wailing, intermingled with gunshots, shouts, and shrieks.

Among the besiegers pandemonium seemed to have broken loose. The house shivered and rang with the awful din.

"That bell! What did it mean?" asked May, wide-eyed with frightened wonder.

"It was the signal agreed on," answered Imbarak from between ashen lips. *"The signal for the massacre!"*

CHAPTER XII.

INTO THE JAWS OF DEATH.

THE Christian world has never forgotten and never will forget the Damascus massacre. Planned as carefully and with as much foresight as any business or political campaign, there was no prearranged detail lacking to complete the carnival of horror which its signal bell inaugurated.

The Damascus nobility, backed by local politicians, and with the undoubted connivance if not help of the city authorities, had for months been preparing the scheme of wholesale murder which was destined to shock the civilized earth.

Damascus Christians had prospered greatly under the lenient rule of the new Sultan.

They had amassed wealth, walked abroad fearlessly, mingled on equal terms with Mohammedans, and had in other ways augmented the already bitter hatred which Moslems entertain toward all races and religions other than their own. The native Jews, too, had come in for their share of the odium.

The nobles and the politicians had cunningly guided the surging tide of popular sentiment into channels that would serve their own purpose. Instead of a hundred street brawls and private assassinations, a general massacre was decreed "In the Name of the Prophet!"

While fanatics rejoiced in the prospect of winning paradise by slaying infidels, the shrewder element of natives looked forward quite as eagerly to rich plunder and the wiping out of old-time grudges.

The nobles and politicians saw the hope of personal aggrandizement, the annexing of their victims' lands and wealth, and the clinching of their own power over the masses. They also perceived an excellent chance to wipe out once and for all a class of citizens who were daily growing more powerful, enjoying the Sultan's protection if not his favor, and who threatened to overthrow the local sway of injustice, tyranny and official lethargy under which Damascus had for centuries labored.

The tocsin bell notified the faithful that the "feast" to which they had been secretly bidden was at last ready. From Katana to the Lebanons flared the fire of massacre.

In less than three days between five and six thousand Christians and Jews lay murdered. The victims' houses were looted and burned, their bodies mutilated, and their names lost from the earth.

Every night the sky-line blazed scarlet with burning villages and with the lurid smoke from a thousand roof-trees. And in world-old Damascus the spirit of murder and rapine stalked abroad. Native Christians and Jews were slaughtered like sheep. Neither bedridden old men nor babies were spared. Such foreigners as had not time to seek refuge in the various embassies shared the fate of their native co-religionists.

The shadow of the Prophet—that gloomy blight which has rested in blessing upon more tragedies than there are stars in the skies— brooded over the stricken city.

Retribution, it is true, was swift and terrible. As soon as loyal troops could be mobilized in the nearest neutral garrisons, the Sultan punished his rebellious nobles as only a Turk knows how to punish.

For months the bodies of the foremost noblemen and politicians who had been engaged in instigating the massacre hung from every branch of great trees in Bazaar Square as a warning to future ill-doers. Their lands and goods were confiscated and their families executed, disgraced or banished. The heirs of the massacred victims were awarded almost any cash damages they might choose to claim, and everything possible was done to remedy their irremediable wrongs.

But this summary justice and generous restitution on the Sultan's part failed to wipe from Turkey's escutcheon the crimson stain that must forever mar its glory.

For a moment after Imbarak's announcement no one spoke. But though the silence of horror gripped the tongues of all the quartet in the darkened room, yet the whole place was alive with sound.

The besiegers had renewed their attacks upon door and windows with redoubled fury. The *imam* was exhorting them piously to begin the "feast" by the slaughter of that particular houseful of unbelievers and renegades.

The desert Bedouins were emptying into the door charge after charge from their long, crooked-stocked flintlocks in the hope of snapping the bolt or weakening the hinges.

And above all rose the querulous treble shriek of the delirious detective in the next room begging for water.

"Oh, my poor uncle!" sobbed May, breaking down all at once. "If only I could be near him to help! And Mrs. Sharpe, too. They will be killed, and I am not there."

"Thank God!" ejaculated Mohun involuntarily.

Then he added: "Don't be afraid for them; it is the lunch hour and they are sure to be at the hotel. The American consulate is in that hotel and the American flag flies over it.

"Even a pack of fanatics will not dare attack the United States consulate. Give yourself no uneasiness; they are safe, but we must look to our own security.

"We have no water, and we are short of provisions. Now that the massacre has begun, there is no hope of a rescue from police or soldiery. We may be cooped up here for weeks. We must not submit to being starved to death or to being driven mad by thirst like poor Shattuck in there. By the way"—addressing Imbarak's mother—"will Shattuck live?"

"As things are now, no. His hurt is not dangerous. It is just a scalp-cut and concussion of the brain. If he had plenty of water to drink he would fall into a perspiration, the fever would break, and in two days he would be well. But without either water or medicine the fever will steadily increase until the brain becomes inflamed, and he will die."

"We must wait until nightfall," decreed Imbarak, "and then take our chances at reaching the fountain under cover of darkness. Not only for the sick man, but for our own sakes. We will all be parched with thirst by that time."

And, indeed, the unwonted exertion and excitement they had all undergone, coupled with the sultry heat of the day and the clouds of dust and powder-smoke sifting into the house at every crevice, had already rendered the whole party excessively thirsty.

"We must bear our thirst until nightfall," said the old woman, "portioning out our one small draft of water among us. We shall suffer from thirst, but the pain must be endured. With the injured American in there it is another matter. Darkness will not fall for six hours. The hottest part of the day is yet to come. Before night the inflammation will have reached his brain, and then it will be too late for mortal help.

"I was a nurse four years at the Beirut hospital, and I know. Without water he must die. If he could have that, he would be on his feet again in three days. But"—with a tinge of apathetic fatalism which characterizes every Oriental—"why talk of that chance? There is no water and he must die."

Mohun went into the next room and leaned over the pallet on which the detective lay. Shattuck was quite delirious. A splash of hectic color dyed his leathery, sallow cheeks, and his brow was burning hot to Ralph's touch. He rolled his head from side to side in the pathetic fashion of cerebral sufferers, and muttered continuously to himself.

Every moment or so he would break off his rambling, senseless monologue to shriek madly for water. His voice was already husky with the dreadful fever, and his lips were cracked and swollen from thirst.

Mohun stood looking down on his fallen enemy, and his face, as May saw it through the doorway, was set and inscrutable. At last he left the invalid and went back to the other room.

"You are certain he cannot recover?" he asked Imbarak's mother.

"Not without water. The fever is already—"

"And with water he has a chance to get well?"

"A chance? He would almost surely make a rapid recovery. But why talk of—"

"Where are you going?" broke in May as Mohun quietly slipped from the room.

He made no reply and she followed him into the stone-paved hallway. Imbarak, seized by a sudden fear, was at her heels.

Ralph had passed to the rear of the hall and was reaching up to a shelf beside the back door whereon stood a line of earthen vessels of varying sizes. Mohun lifted three of the largest of these vessels to the floor and began attaching to them the primitive yoke from which Syrian housewives hang water-jars in order to carry them to the wells or fountains.

Divining his guest's purpose, Imbarak sprang forward, horrified.

"*Howaji!*" he cried. "You would not—surely you do not contemplate this insane deed?"

"Unbar the back door for me, Imbarak," requested Mohun coolly, as he adjusted the yoke to his shoulders, "and try to keep the people on the roofs busy by pumping away at them through the loopholes with the Winchesters until I get back."

The groom threw himself between Ralph and the barred door.

"It is madness!" he declared hotly. "What is that wounded police agent to you that you should lose your life in an attempt to get him water? Let him die. He came here to destroy you. Let him die, I say!"

"Let me go, Imbarak!" commanded Mohun, and there was a note of stern imperiousness in his voice before which Imbarak gave back. "Unbar the door for me. It is not only for the detective but for all of us that I am going."

"If any one must go, let it be I," urged the anguished groom.

"Imbarak," retorted Mohun coldly, "if you block my path longer I shall be compelled to force my way out. It would pain me to raise my hand against a man who has served me so well. Therefore—"

With a sobbing, choked expletive of despair, the groom bent himself to the task of unbarring the door.

Mohun came close to the entrance, prepared to make a dash for the fountain the instant the last bolt should be withdrawn, but again he met with an obstacle.

A light hand was laid on his arm, grasping his sleeve with nervous intensity, and May Farrar confronted him. Her face was white and drawn, her big eyes ablaze as she clung to the rash adventurer's arm and opposed her frail strength to his.

"How dare you?" she whispered, voiceless with the intensity of her emotion. "How *dare* you throw your life away like this?"

Tears, entreaties, even hysterics would not have astonished Mohun in the least, but the concentrated anger in the girl's voice left him dumfounded.

"You shall not go!" she resumed indignantly. "You may think it a fine thing to lose your life in this spectacular way, but you have no right to leave us like this. You shall *not*."

"Miss Farrar," he answered, recovering from his surprise, "my life is mine. I have not noticed that any one else has placed a fictitious valuation on it, and I am certain *I* do not.

"We must have water not only for Shattuck but for ourselves. If not, none of our lives will be worth very much by the time we've endured another twenty-four hours of thirst. Please stand aside and let me go."

"I will *not.*"

She stood squarely in front of him, meeting his compelling glance with one of agonized rebellion against his resolve.

She could scarcely have analyzed her own emotions, yet she was stirred to the very soul with the longing and determination to save this man from the self-destruction which he was courting. It was a battle of wills, and it raged with a fierce vehemence until suddenly the girl's eyes faltered and fell and she broke into a fit of passionate weeping.

Lifting her tenderly to one side, Mohun turned to the door just as the last bolt was drawn and the final barrier removed.

"To the loophole with your Winchester and keep them busy!" he shouted to Imbarak, and bounded quickly through the doorway into the carefully watched garden.

CHAPTER XIII.

TO STARVE THEM OUT.

AS in his two former sorties, Mohun relied on the audacity and the element of unexpectedness to aid his plan. Here, at the rear of the beleaguered house whose front the mob was assailing, the handful of armed men who had been stationed on the adjoining roofs did not expect any of the defenders to emerge so soon into the garden. They counted, of course, on the inmates being eventually driven by thirst to attempt a passage to the fountain, but they did not expect such a move until nightfall.

The men sat on the roofs, guns across knees, gossiping or watching the red tongues of incendiary flame that were already beginning to shoot up from point to point along the hazy sky-line.

They remained on the roofs instead of joining the more exciting attack from the street, on the off-chance that a face or figure might be carelessly exposed in one of the house-windows long enough to present a target. But a rush for the fountain was the last thing anticipated.

Hence Mohun, making a dash from door to fountain, had covered the entire distance—perhaps ninety feet—before a yell from the roofs told that his presence was discovered.

There was not a patch of cover in the whole garden that would have hidden a boy of ten.

The American was thus exposed to the fire of every rifle on the rooftops during the really momentary but seemingly eternal time it took him to submerge the three great *ghoolas* (native water-jars) into the pool of the fountain.

The jars, being wide of mouth, filled almost simultaneously, and, working with consummate haste yet with perfect self-possession, Mohun clapped on the pigskin lids, raised the yoke to his shoulders and began his return trip. From the second that the cry from the opposite roof had awakened the whole group of guards to the fact that one of the besieged had left the house, the dozen or more natives who leaned from the surrounding parapets had opened fire on the daring American.

That he had not fallen at the first irregular volley was due to several fortunate chances—the surprise and haste that unsettled the marksmen's aim, the antique and defective style of their weapons, the confusing and illusive swirl of spray from the fountain that danced between Ralph and his antagonists.

Most important of all, Imbarak's bullets raked the three parapets mercilessly, driving back some of their occupants, causing others to duck for shelter, and unsettling the aim of the remainder.

One man pitched forward from the opposite roof and fell with a crash among the rose-bushes at the farther end of the garden. Another reeled back out of sight, his teeth clenched in death agony.

A third let his rifle clatter over the side of the parapet as he fell to nursing a smashed wrist.

But Mohun's return journey from the fountain was by no means as swift as had been his outward rush. Each of the three huge jars held five gallons of water, making an aggregate load, apart from the weight of the heavy *ghoolas* themselves, of at least one hundred and twenty pounds.

Bullet after bullet whizzed past him, raising tiny puffs of dust from the ground or flattening with a vicious "spat-t-t!" against the stucco walls of the house.

The journey he had traversed in less than four seconds on the way out now seemed to stretch away into miles. No one who has not been under fire can realize the awful strain it throws on the nerves, and the almost irresistible desire to cast away every impediment and run to shelter.

Long as the return trip seemed to Mohun, it was a thousand times longer to the girl who, regardless of personal danger, watched him from the half-open doorway of the house.

With her hands clenched until the blood oozed from the finger-tips, her blanched lips moving mechanically in wordless prayer, May Farrar awaited the return of the man who, as she now acknowledged even to herself, was supreme master of her heart and mind.

As Mohun gained the threshold a bullet struck one of the jars full in the center.

The stout earthen receptacle shivered into twenty pieces, the water falling in a cascade about the overburdened man, to be sucked up greedily by the sun-parched earth.

With his two remaining full *ghoolas* Mohun gained the cool shelter of the passageway, where May closed and barred the door behind him.

During the afternoon, night, and all the following morning the street and roofs were choked with howling natives, mad for vengeance and murder. When some would depart to take their share in scenes of easier slaughter and plunder in various parts of the city, others took their places.

During the first few hours repeated attempts had been made to storm the place, but the little house was stanch and the implements in the hands of the besiegers were primitive.

The space between the courtyard wall and the front door of the house was too shallow to permit of the manipulation of a log or timber sufficiently long and heavy to serve as a battering-ram. Moreover, the besieged kept up so effective a fire from the shutter loopholes that the courtyard was more than once strewn with dead Moslems. Therefore, their first wild rage succumbing to the calculating, undying purpose so peculiar to the Oriental temperament, the besiegers ceased their efforts to carry the place by attack and resolved to allow a stronger ally to do their fighting for them.

They knew that the inmates of the house, not having been prepared for a siege, were doubtless very lightly provisioned, and that although the problem of thirst had been temporarily solved, the equally potent problem of hunger must soon confront them in all its irresistible force.

So, while guarding the place jealously, they refrained from exposing themselves to needles chances of death and waited calmly to starve out the little garrison.

Within the house matters were fast approaching a grave crisis. Zenas Shattuck, thanks to the timely arrival of the two jars of water and to the old Syrian woman's skilled nursing, was infinitely better.

The fever had been quelled, the brain was clear again, and the scalp wound was doing well. The detective was still weak, but bade fair to be on his feet in a day or two.

Meantime, though receiving every necessary attention, he was otherwise ignored by everybody.

Imbarak had informed him in a few curt sentences the risk Mohun had taken on his account and that he owed his life to his proposed victim's heroism. Zenas had received the information with a non-committal grunt and had not spoken a word to any one since then.

Mohun and Imbarak had, after the latter's return from the garden, taken a full and exact inventory of their stock of food. They found that by serving half-rations there were enough provisions in the house to last May, the old woman and the wounded detective for two days.

The two young men resolved to eat nothing themselves.

In order to prevent the others from discovering this ruse, they always made a feint of carrying their share of the daily rations to their separate points of duty, whence they later sought an opportunity of restoring the food untasted to the common stock.

The besiegers, realizing the hunger of the defenders, made a point of eating heartily just outside the house, and once roasted an ox, whole, in the street, where the fumes of the cooking meat could be wafted to the nostrils of the starving garrison.

And so the first twenty-four hours of the siege dragged along, each hour bringing near a denouement which not even the fanatical assailants themselves could have anticipated.

CHAPTER XIV.

THE TRUTH AT LAST.

IT was the afternoon of the second day. For forty-eight hours neither Mohun nor Imbarak had tasted food.

Ralph, being the more powerfully built of the two, showed more outward signs of the deprivation. His eyes were sunken and blood-shot, and dark circles had formed beneath them; his face was drawn and haggard, his lips tight-set.

Imbarak had just awakened from an hour of heavy sleep and had relieved Ralph as sentry at the front of the house.

Mohun passed through the large living-room on his way to his own sleeping apartment at the rear. The groom's mother was dressing Shattuck's wound on the other side of the passageway and May sat alone in the living-room. The strain of the past two days had left its mark on May Farrar's face as well as on Mohun's. Her cheeks had lost their color and contour, and there was an alert, tense air about her.

But a greater, subtler change had come over the girl. A new, soft light shone in her dark eyes; there was a gentler cadence to her voice and an unaccustomed humility in her proud bearing.

As Ralph entered the room she glanced up from her task of oiling and cleaning several reserve weapons, and greeted him with a sweet shyness foreign to her old self.

"You must be tired out," she said. "Is there any sign of their raising the siege?"

"None," he answered drearily. "They don't attack because they know they can win more cheaply by starving us. From time to time recruits from other parts of the city join them. Imbarak has overheard their talk, and from what they say there can be no doubt that the massacre is general. But—"

"Ralph," she said, looking him in the eyes, a sudden resolve possessing her, "please tell me the truth. I can bear it better than suspense. Is there *any* hope for us?

"No"—as he hesitated—"you must not try to put me off; it is kinder to tell me frankly. I shall know then what to expect. Shall we leave here alive?"

"We are in God's hands," answered Ralph simply.

There was a pause, then a long-drawn sigh from the girl.

"That means there is no mortal hope?" she asked.

He had not the heart to deceive her, so made no reply, but stood looking down at the brave, beautiful face upraised to his own.

"Life is very sweet," she said, with a little catch in her breath, "and I am young. It seems hard to leave everything, doesn't it?"

There was no fear, no repining in her tone—nothing but a sort of awed wonder, tinged with regret.

"We shall do our best for you. You know that," replied Ralph, at a loss for words.

"As if I could doubt you!" she said in gentle reproof. "Do you remember," she added, "that evening in the hotel courtyard the day I came to Damascus, where you warned me of the danger and when I behaved so horribly to you and ungratefully?

"Do you remember you told me that when the real danger came you would be at my side to die for me? I was angry at you then, and I had forced myself to distrust you, and yet through it all I felt happier and safer somehow for your words. Wasn't it strange?"

A lump rose in Mohun's throat. Strain and starvation had weakened his iron nerves. He sought to turn the talk from her to himself.

"You speak of your anger and distrust as though they were things of the past," he said. "If they were merited at that time, they are still merited. I have done nothing to clear myself in your eyes—nothing that materially affects the true state of things nor that wipes out the fact that I am a fugitive from justice and—"

"Hush!" begged the girl, tears brimming in her eyes as she spoke. "You mustn't say such things of yourself. Would a felon or a coward have acted as you have done in the past two days? If all the world rose to condemn you, I should *know* you were not guilty."

"Thank you," he muttered, his face averted.

She followed him as he moved toward the shuttered window, and spoke again, earnestly, as she gained his side.

"Ralph," she begged, "I don't know why you refused to tell me why you had fled from home and why you refused to return to face the law. But I know now that your reason, whatever it was, was a good one, and that you acted for the best. I trust you implicitly, you see.

"But"—with a nervous laugh—"I am a woman, and therefore curious. No, it isn't mere curiosity, either. I don't know just *what* it is. But won't you tell me now why you left America and the truth about the whole mystery?"

She saw his face change and read the unspoken refusal in his eyes, but she went on quickly:

"You say yourself that we shall never leave this house alive, so your secret could not escape even though I chose to reveal it. Anything that is said here can make no difference to others nor be a breach of trust.

"Don't you understand? This house is like the grave—it guards its secrets forever. Knowing yourself absolved from your duty to outsiders, can't you grant me this one favor? The last, perhaps, that—"

"Yes!"

His reply, curt and decided, broke in upon her plea. The suddenness and unexpectedness of his concession caused her a decided sensation of surprise.

There was a note of glad relief in his words as he repeated:

"Yes, you are right. Whatever is said here can go no further, and you cannot dream of what a joy, what a comfort it will be to me to set myself straight with you.

"I feel now I have this right, and that right reconciles me to our hopeless position. For if there were a ghost of a chance that we should leave here alive I could not speak—even to you. Ah, if you could know how I have longed to tell you, to make you see I am not the blackguard you have thought me—"

"Don't!" she begged, pained at the memories he evoked.

"I didn't blame you, even when your scorn cut me most keenly," he answered. "My actions must all have seemed those of a scoundrel. Looking back over it all, it may be I acted foolishly. But in moments of stress one must do what just then seems best.

"I am not referring to anything that has happened here in Syria, but back in Boston. My knocking Shattuck down that night in Jerusalem and my dodging him ever since were part of a needful program, as you will see."

He paused as though marshaling the facts of his forthcoming story in correct order. May waited, afraid to break in on his thoughts by a word or gesture.

From the half-moon loophole of the shutter a glint of sunlight fell across his haggard, powder-streaked face, and she read there deep marks of suffering for which the events of the siege did not account.

When he spoke it was in a level, emotionless voice:

"You remember Mark Warren, of course? He was often at your father's house when you were a child."

"Mr. Warren? Of course I remember him! He and my uncle were dear friends and he stayed with us whenever he came to New York. We haven't seen anything of him for the past ten years or so, as he is a good deal of an invalid and never travels. But how did *you* know he was a friend of Uncle Jack's?"

"Because I have not only heard him speak of your uncle a thousand times, but I came with him once to your house, twelve years ago."

"You came with him?" echoed May incredulously.

"Yes. You were a little eight-year-old girl then, and I only saw you at meals. I—"

The sudden memory of a face flashed across May Farrar's mind— the tanned face of an overgrown, bashful boy. She recalled where she had last seen it and how intently she had stared at the lad in the hope of making him blush.

"It was twelve or thirteen years ago," she said, voicing her thoughts aloud, "in our dining-room in New York. The boy was sitting next to—"

"To Mr. Mark Warren. I am his son, Bayard."

"Bayard Warren! *You?* A dozen times something in your face has struck me as familiar, yet I could never place it. And you are Bayard Warren? But how—"

"How did I happen to take the name of Ralph Mohun? That is part of the story."

"Go on please. I won't interrupt you again if I can help it."

"My father was at the head of one of the largest banking firms in Boston. When I left Harvard four years ago I went to work for him. His health was failing, and last year he made me his partner. The firm became Warren & Son.

"From the first I saw my father's ill-health was beginning to have an effect on his formerly splendid business ability. He took to making rash speculations, to risking the firm's name in ventures that a few years earlier he would have known were unsafe. Only by the combined efforts of the old cashier and myself did we escape financial shipwreck. Van Zandt, the cashier, had been with my father for thirty years and knew every detail of the business as well as he.

"With Van Zandt's help I kept things going; and understand, please"—he broke of with concern—"that I am not blaming my father in the least. He was a peerless financier and a man of the most upright business integrity when he was in his prime. But ill-health and increasing age combined to shake his splendid faculties and to make him do things he would never have dreamed of doing had he been himself."

"I understand," said the girl gently.

"Van Zandt told me of my father's eccentricities when I first entered the firm. He explained it all as considerately as possible and showed me the various risky ventures in which the poor old gentleman had been dabbling. Van Zandt said he hated to tell all this, even to me, for he loved my father like a brother.

"But he said my knowledge and aid were necessary in order to help him keep the firm from disaster. At last came the crash."

He stopped again, and May, looking into his face, saw the corners of his mouth twitch convulsively. His nerves were unstrung, and the story he was telling evidently drew heavily on them.

"Little by little," he went on, "money disappeared from our reserve fund. First in small sums, then in larger, until our reserve was practically wiped out. My father, Van Zandt and I were the only persons who had access to that fund.

"Van Zandt came to me one night with tears in his eyes. Weeping like a child, the faithful old cashier showed me the ledgers that indicated the loss. By studying them I saw, in my father's own handwriting, the story of his fall. In order to get money for speculations which he knew the firm would not sanction, he had little by little withdrawn money from the reserve, masking the deficits by small entries.

"Van Zandt showed me, too, my father's private note-book, showing in what crazy transactions each separate sum had been squandered. The proof was there, in my father's own hand.

"I had been warned by Van Zandt for nearly a year of my father's failing health and its effect on his mind. Yet the shock of knowing—actually *knowing*—that he had so far lost his great mental powers and his unswerving sense of right as to stoop to such deceptions and petty dishonesty well-nigh drove me mad.

"It seems he had sent in panic for Van Zandt and made a clean breast of the whole thing, giving him the notebook and ledger, frankly confessing that he himself could not unravel the tangle, and begging old Van to save him. He also entreated him not to tell me, saying he could not bear his son's contempt.

"Well, Van Zandt and I worked all night on the situation. The longer we worked the more hopeless we saw it was. The reserve fund was gone. Our clients' money was squandered. It was only a matter of a few days before the whole thing must come out. My father would stand in the felon's dock—would go to prison for embezzlement. The disgrace and confinement would kill him as surely as would a dose of poison. If we could but gain a few months' time we could realize on some of the firm's own investments, pay back the reserve and reestablish the business.

"This Van Zandt was sure could be done, but fully three months would be required in which to accomplish it, and exposure could not be staved off for more than a week at most.

"The next day, saying not a word of my intention, and leaving only a note of explanation for Van Zandt in which I told him to make my reasons clear to my father, I withdrew the few hundreds I had of my own from the bank and fled secretly from Boston."

"You mean," interposed the girl, "that you ran away in order to give the impression that it was you and not your father who had embezzled the money? You went because you knew that when the exposure came suspicion would attach itself to the man who had run away?"

Ralph nodded acquiescence.

"But," urged the girl, "why didn't you send Mr. Van Zandt away instead? If he was so devoted to your father's interests—"

"Because no one but Van Zandt had the experience and the commercial acumen necessary for putting the firm on its feet after the exposure. If it were thought that I alone was guilty, my father's business credit would not suffer.

"Hence either Van Zandt or I, the only two others who had access to the reserve fund, must go. Indeed, it was old Van himself who, inadvertently, gave me the idea of running away. In the course of our talk he said he should have done so himself were it not that no one but he could readjust the wrecked firm."

"But why didn't you speak personally to your father about it? Surely—"

"He was very ill and nervously upset. Besides, he had used Van Zandt as an intermediary between us because he could not bear to face me. My pride, too, was hurt by that.

"Moreover, I knew he would not permit his son to make such a sacrifice for him. After I should be gone, Van Zandt could persuade him to be quiet and to realize I had acted for the best."

"But you should have seen him, nevertheless," persisted May. "There might have been some mistake."

"The whole terrible story, in my father's own handwriting, was in the ledger and note-book," said Ralph sadly. "I crossed the ocean, with no clear idea I would be followed. My only plan was to remain in hiding in some out-of-the-way corner of the world for three months or so, until I should receive a cablegram from Van Zandt that it was safe to return.

"I knew that until that cablegram should be received the firm would not be on its feet again. It wasn't until that night in Jerusalem that I realized the police were really on my track. I knew Shattuck well by sight. He had been one of our clients at the bank. He is reputed the cleverest thief-taker in all New England. But how he learned I was in Syria I can't imagine. When I met you in Cairo I demurred at first at the idea of joining your party. But it seemed so safe, and I was fairly *hungry* for the society of people in my own walk of life. Besides—"

He checked himself sharply, but the look in his hollow, bloodshot eyes told May more clearly than any words just what had been the real temptation that had made him attach himself to their company.

"Do you know," she said, after a short silence, "I think you are the bravest, noblest man I have ever met. You are a hero of the truest sort. I have no words," she ended confusedly, "to tell you how I honor you. But why didn't you tell me the story before?"

"Because Van Zandt and I had exchanged solemn promises not to breathe the real truth about the embezzlement to a living soul.

"We stand to-day in the shadow of death, you and I, and I hold myself absolved of that promise.

"When Shattuck confronted me in Jerusalem I knew I must not let him capture me. For if he did, and if I returned before the bank was firm again, my whole flight would have been fruitless and my father's guilt would have come to light.

"I saw I must keep out of the way until I learned definitely that affairs were readjusted. I could not have acted otherwise, could I?"

"And every word of my cruel reproaches must have been doubly bitter because so utterly undeserved. I can never, *never* forgive myself. Why did you risk your life for such a wicked, ungrateful girl as I?"

He looked her fairly in the eyes.

"I think you know why," he replied, and her glance fell before his, while her heart throbbed wildly in expectation of the words she was sure were about to follow.

"I think you know," he repeated, "and I *hope* you do, for I have not the right to tell you even now. In the eyes of the world a stain still rests on my name, and no true man can say what I am yearning to unless he can offer with the words something besides the smirched reputation of a fugitive from justice."

"Very interestin'," commented a croaking voice behind them.

Turning with a start, Ralph noticed that Zenas Shattuck had crawled from his pallet in the hall to the doorway of the living-room and had evidently overheard the whole conversation.

"Very interestin' story," continued the detective blandly, oblivious of the unfriendly looks cast upon him; "so interestin', in fact, that it seems 'most a pity that there ain't a word of truth in the whole of it."

CHAPTER XV.

THE LAST STAND.

THE siege wore on for another full day with little change from without.

But on the morning of the third day it became evident that something new was afoot. A native, dusty and sweating from a long run, dashed up to the throng in the street and shouted some indistinct tidings which even Imbarak's ear could not catch.

The effect on the mob was electrical. A fury seized them, and their confused shouts and gesticulations showed that the news, whatever it was, had changed the stolid patience in which they awaited the starving of their victims into a whirlwind of wrathful frenzy.

One big man sprang on a refuse pile and made a short, impassioned speech, at whose conclusion a dozen or so natives began at once to shake out the contents of their powder-horns into a common heap.

"This is the end, *howaji!*" muttered Imbarak, who had caught enough of the brief harangue to understand its import. "Something, I know not what, has occurred to make haste necessary. They will wait no longer, but blow in the front door with powder, and rush us."

Even as he spoke men were dashing to and fro between the door and the pile of powder. Ralph snatched up his rifle and turned to the loophole.

"It is useless, *howaji,*" said Imbarak in a heavy voice that proved he was fast falling under the hopeless spell of oriental fatalism; "they are too many. We might kill two or three, but already enough powder is at the threshold to blow the door to atoms."

"Quick, then!" ordered Ralph, shaking off the inertia bred of starvation and fatigue. "Up-stairs to the loft, all of you except Imbarak! "

His plan was the last hopeless idea of a desperate man—to put Zenas and the two women in the loft, and for himself and Imbarak to defend the narrow stone stairway leading to the upper floor as long as they could.

He briefly outlined his plan, and, to his surprise, Shattuck offered to remain on the stairs. To this Ralph opposed a decided refusal.

He had noted the narrowness of the stairway and had seen that no more than two men could fight to advantage, side by side, in that confined space. A third would be an encumbrance. He briefly explained, adding:

"Take care of the women. If there is a chance of saving them, you can be of more use up there than on the stairs."

The women silently obeyed his orders and followed Shattuck to the loft. May came last.

As she passed Ralph on the stairs she paused and seemed about to speak, but her heart was too full for words. After one long, silent glance she continued her ascent.

Imbarak, meanwhile, had been reloading every revolver and the two guns, and had placed them, with the small store of the remaining ammunition, at the top of the stairway.

He and Ralph next threw two straw mattresses across the upper part of the flight to serve as buttresses. Imbarak had just sprung down the stairs for a third when with a blinding flash the charge of powder placed against the outer door was exploded.

The house rocked with the impact and every window-pane shivered. More than half-way up the stairs Ralph was almost knocked down by the explosion's jar, but quickly recovered himself, and with leveled Winchester awaited the rush that he knew must follow.

As he did so he was aware of Imbarak. The groom had been perilously near the door. The explosion had hurled him, senseless and bruised, across the lowest step.

Ralph was about to leap the mattress-barrier and run down to his aid, but he saw that it was too late.

With a howl of fanatical triumph the mob surged in through the shattered doorway. In less than a second the whole lower floor was alive with blood-mad men.

Ralph saw that he had done wisely in not attempting to hold the ground floor against their onset. Here on the landing he might keep them at bay for a few minutes.

A shout proclaimed the discovery of his presence behind the barrier. A half-dozen men leaped up the stairway, while twenty more sent a scattering volley of bullets and slugs into the mattresses.

"If I die, I'll die like a man—worthy of her!" thought Ralph as he pumped bullet after bullet into the enemy. The fierce joy of battle was hot upon him, crushing back hunger and weakness.

He laughed loudly as he pumped the stream of leaden death at his foes.

In a moment the stairway was a horrible shamble, choked with dead and dying. In that narrow space scarcely two could climb abreast, and the high-power bullets drilled their way through two and three men, one behind the other, before losing velocity. The mad, murderous rush halted.

The mob snarled and shrieked about the foot of the stairs, but none sought to attempt that death-swept ascent.

Shot after shot they fired, but the top of the stairs was thick with powder-smoke, and, except for a bullet graze across the cheek, Ralph crouched unharmed behind his mattress barricade.

Then an order was given below, and suddenly a dozen flaming particles of cloth and paper were hurled upward against the mattresses. The inflammable material caught fire at once and blazed up, its smoke nearly stifling the helpless Mohun.

A yell of delight from the assailants, and more flaming particles were tossed upward.

Ralph kicked aside his blazing and useless defenses, and, a pistol in either hand (for his rifle was now empty), stood awaiting his death.

The mob gathered for a rush. The feet of the foremost were on the lowest step of the corpse-strewn stairs.

A cry of fear, not of exultation like the sounds that had hitherto deafened the defenders, rang from the doorway.

A sentence in Arabic was shouted in shrill warning from the courtyard. A clatter of horses' hoofs sounded from the street.

In an instant the whole house was clear of natives.

Ralph, uncomprehending, watched his late foes flying madly along the dusty thoroughfare. He staggered to the foot of the stairs for a closer view. Down the Street of the Mehdan tore a squadron of Syrian light cavalry, in hot pursuit of the scattered fanatics.

The Damascus massacre was at an end.

The besiegers, hearing rumors of the soldiers' arrival in town, had hurried to crush the plucky defense of the little household.

But they had been too late by one brief minute to accomplish their murderous purpose.

Imbarak, recovering from his swoon, was rising weakly to his feet as Ralph reentered the house. Mohun passed him, ran up-stairs and tried the loft-door. To his surprise, it yielded to his touch.

"We're safe!" he panted as he entered. Then he paused in dismay on the threshold.

The loft was empty!

The trap-door leading to the roof was open, but a hasty survey of the neighboring housetops showed no signs of the loft's late occupants.

"Those devils broke in through the scuttle and carried them off!" cried Ralph, running dizzily back to the street.

A man in native dress, ragged, bloodstained, reeling from weakness, pushed his way past servants and idlers along the entrance of the Hotel Basraoul and rushed into the great reception hall where the United States consul had his headquarters.

The room was full of people, but the intruder did not heed them. He went straight to a desk near the door and, addressing an official seated there, said hoarsely in English:

"A lady, the niece of an American army officer, has been kidnaped by natives and—"

A long, lean man detached himself from the crowd about the center of the room, slouched forward and, laying his hand on the newcomer's shoulder, drawled:

"Bayard Warren, I arrest you in the name of the Commonwealth of Massachusetts, on a warrant charging you with embezzlement of funds belonging to the banking firm of Warren & Son. I—"

"Never mind that now!" shouted Ralph impatiently. "Where's Miss Farrar? What have—"

"We heard the front door give way," replied Zenas, "and she fainted. I picked her up and brought her here over the roofs. I was dressed like a heathen and they didn't stop me—thought I'd captured her, I s'pose. She's all right. She came to by the time I'd got her here. I've sent for her, and for some one else," he added with a chuckle, looking at Ralph significantly.

Ralph's relief took the form of sudden weakness. He staggered and sank into the nearest chair.

"I've arrested ye, young man," went on Zenas, "because I swore I'd do it. But I ain't cur enough to nab a man that's saved my life. I'd have let you go before we got to America, even if—even if we'd had to take that trip together—which we haven't."

"I don't understand," faltered Ralph.

"No? Well, there's the explanation." Shattuck pointed to two men and a woman who were entering the room.

One of the men Ralph recognized as Major Crawford. The girl, he saw with a thrill of ungovernable joy, was May Farrar.

But as he looked at the third member of the party—a white-bearded, feeble man of seventy—a mist swam before his eyes.

"Father!" he muttered uncertainly, and would have fallen but for Shattuck's supporting arm.

When he had been revived he learned, little by little, the reason for the elder Warren's presence there.

"It wasn't a week after you sailed," explained the old man after tenderly reproaching his son for the uneasiness he had caused, "before detectives I had put on the case brought me indisputable evidence of Van Zandt's guilt. I was thunderstruck, for I had trusted him in everything.

"When the fellow saw he was cornered he confessed he'd been robbing the firm for over a year. He went on to tell how he had covered his trail by telling you abominable lies about my speculations. Speculations! I never speculated in my life.

"He even confessed how he had copied my handwriting in the ledger and note-book and shown them to you as proofs of my feeble-mindedness and dishonesty.

"It seems he cooked up your flight to give him time to get away while the police were looking for you. He had set Shattuck on your trail the very day before we arrested him. He is a clever man, is Van Zandt, but he'll have to exercise his cleverness behind bars for a few years, I fancy."

"But the firm? "

"The firm was never in real danger. The moment I heard Van Zandt's confession I set out to look for you, and a pretty race you led me! I arrived here on the day the massacre began, just an hour after Miss Farrar left the hotel to hunt you up."

Night had fallen before Ralph was strong enough to rise. He crossed the moonlit courtyard of the hotel toward the sumptuous apartments occupied by his father.

The fountain plashed in the center of the court; the fragrance of orange flowers was heavy on the air; a nightingale sang its heart out in the branches of a neighboring rose-tree.

As Ralph passed a stone bench in the court a white-gowned, slender figure rose from it and came gracefully forward to meet him.

"I was waiting for you," said May Farrar, a little tremulously.

He stopped and gazed speechlessly at her as she stood bathed in the soft moonlight.

Now that all barriers between were removed, he could find no words.

"Dear," went on the girl in feigned anger, "are you actually going to force me to propose to you?"

With an articulate cry he caught her slight form in his arms.

"My darling! Oh, my darling!" he murmured brokenly.

THE END.

Appendix

Publication information
for the stories
in this book

The Fugitive

was serialized in four issues of Argosy, from August through November of 1905:

August, 1905	Chapters I to IV
September, 1905	Chapters V to VIII
October, 1905	Chapters IX to XII
November, 1905	Chapters XIII to XV

Argosy, August 1905

Front text:

A modern romance in the Holy Land, involving the mystery of an American who seems to be a villain, and culminating in the massacre at Damascus.

Argosy, September 1905

Front text:

A modern romance in the Holy Land, involving the mystery of an American who seems to be a villain, and culminating in the massacre at Damascus.

SYNOPSIS OF CHAPTERS PREVIOUSLY PUBLISHED.

MAJOR CRAWFORD and his niece, May Farrar, are traveling through the Orient. On the way they are joined by Sir Arthur Cole, and Ralph Mohun, an American. Mohun rescues May and his own groom, Imbarak, from death in the quicksands, and thereby wins May's unconfessed love and the lifelong gratitude of Imbarak, who informs Mohun of the pending Christian massacre in Damascus, warning him to prevent Major Crawford's party from visiting that city. Mohun openly avoids Miss Farrar until they arrive at Jerusalem, where Zenas Shattuck, a Boston detective, appears and arrests Mohun, who breaks away from him and escapes.

May Farrar, unable to sleep after the evening's excitement, makes an early journey to the Garden of Gethsemane. Here she meets Mohun disguised as an Oriental beggar. He warns her not to go to Damascus, and refuses to tell her the reason for his arrest, saying that he is guilty but must not be brought to punishment. At this point Shattuck arrives, and is deceived by Mohun's disguise. May, angered by Ralph's attempt to escape, resolves to force him to take the right step, and as Shattuck is about to send the supposed beggars about their business interrupts their flight with:

"Mr. Shattuck, you have been deceived."

* This story began in the August issue of THE ARGOSY, which will be mailed to any address on receipt of 10 cents.

Argosy, October 1905

Front text:

A modern romance in the Holy Land, involving the mystery of an American who seems to be a villain, and culminating in the massacre at Damascus.

SYNOPSIS OF CHAPTERS PREVIOUSLY PUBLISHED.

MAJOR CRAWFORD and his niece, May Farrar, are traveling through the Orient. On the way they are joined by Sir Arthur Cole, and Ralph Mohun, an American. Mohan rescues May and his own groom, Imbarak, from death in the quicksands, and thereby wins May's unconfessed love and the lifelong gratitude of Imbarak, who informs Mohun of the pending Christian massacre in Damascus, warning him to prevent Major Crawford's party from visiting that city. Mohun openly avoids Miss Farrar until they arrive at Jerusalem, where Zenas Shattuck, a Boston detective, appears and arrests Mohun, who breaks away from him and escapes.

May Farrar, unable to sleep after the evening's excitement, makes an early journey to the Garden of Gethsemane. Here she meets Mohun disguised as an Oriental beggar. He warns her not to go to Damascus, and refuses to tell her the reason for his arrest, saying that he is guilty but must not be brought to punishment. At this point Shattuck arrives, and Mohun is obliged to leave the garden.

In spite of the warning, the major's party enters Damascus. Mohun is also there, and May learns that he is living at Imbarak's home.

Shattuck appears in the city disguised, and May, accompanied by Sir Arthur, visits Mohun to warn him of the detective's presence. While she is within the house, Sir Arthur is annoyed by some loungers. He strikes one and a riot follows; but he manages to escape just as May closes the door of Imbarak's house behind her, to find herself in the midst of a frenzied mob.

*This story began in the August issue of The ARGOSY. The two back numbers will be mailed to any address on. receipt of 20 cents,

Argosy, November 1905

Front text:
A modern romance in the Holy Land, involving the mystery of an American who seems to be a villain, and culminating in the massacre at Damascus.

*This story began in the August issue of THE ARGOSY. The three back numbers will be mailed to any address on receipt of 30 cents.

Forty Ali Babas and a Thief

was published complete in the September 19, 1914 issue of All-Story Cavalier Weekly.

Front text:
Author of "Articles of War," "The Sword of Ali Diab," "Dad," etc.

Editorial changes:
Van Cleek Duyck was in one instance referred to as "Dr. Duyck." In all other cases, he was a "Mr." Lacking any indication that he was a physician or had earned a PhD, that one instance was editorially changed to "Mr. Duyck."

General Note:
The total number of "Ali Baba" rugs, given in the title and confirmed in the story, is forty. Also quite plain is the number of such rugs sold by Brenner—twelve. Yet, the number of unsold rugs is ambiguous.

Other books available
from the
Silver Creek Press

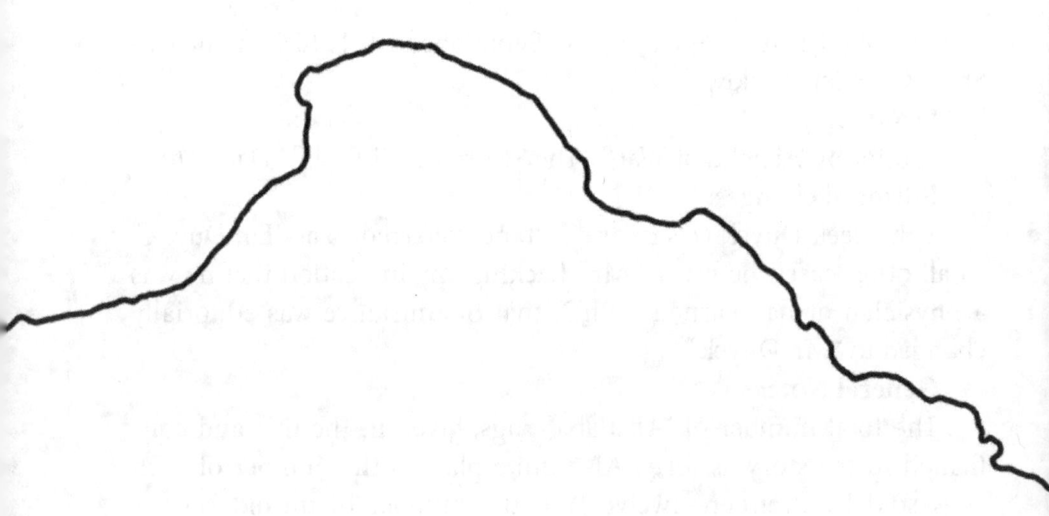

The
Albert Payson Terhune Reader
Series

Each reprints over 20 stories by Terhune
from pulp magazines of the 1900s through the 1920s,
with all original illustrations.

Other fiction by Terhune

The Flood Fighters
In Treason's Track
The White Way
First book publication for each

Historical Essays by Terhune

The Woman Tamers

Cheddar Cheese
by Francis Lynde

All books are available from
major bookstores online,
as print books and as e-books.

www.ingramcontent.com/pod-product-compliance
Lightning Source LLC
Chambersburg PA
CBHW071003180726
48291CB00004B/1411

Forty Ali Babas and a Thief

Forty Ali Babas and a Thief

SCP Tête-Bêche
Book 1

CHAPTER I.

"I'm a Bargain."

"HOW did you get in here?" demanded Ulrich Laing, glowering up from a maelstrom of papers that swirled across the surface of his table-desk.

The visitor did not reply to the stark question. Instead, he glanced carelessly back toward the half-open door of the inner office, then down at his own well-shod feet, and continued his leisurely advance toward the desk.

Laing half rose to his feet. The newcomer's advance had neither the bravado of a crank or creditor nor the temerity of a canvasser who has won his way through forbidden portals.

And Laing, who knew something of men, was mildly puzzled. Perhaps that was why his pudgy hand halted on its journey toward the desk-bell. The visitor had halted at the far side of the desk, as though courteously waiting an invitation to sit down.

As his involuntary host did not offer such invitation, but continued to glare at him with puzzled query, the stranger whiled away the momentary pause by glancing about the room.

It was perhaps the most unusually furnished private office in New York. Its appointments might well have been epitomized in one word—rugs.

Rugs covered the floor, to the blotting out of any view of parquetry or other basic flooring. Rugs lining the walls to the topmost molding, obliterating wainscot, baseboard, and all else.

Of the four chairs, two served as "horses" for rugs.

And in the heart of it all—the desk-center was a ten by eighteen-inch Persian "foot-rug" of unbelievable antiquity—sat Ulrich Laing, the "rug king," foremost rug-dealer and expert of the New World; a man whose rugs were his religion as well as his fortune.

The brief, appraising glance of inspection over, the intruder again met Laing's lowering gaze. The rug king noted that the man's look was level, self-possessed, without a hint of effrontery, and wholly unafraid.

"I asked you," repeated Laing, "how you came here."

"Obviously," returned the other, "through the door. The one just behind me. That one."

"Naturally," sniffed Laing in elephantine sarcasm, "that one. Since it's the only one leading into this room. But now that you're here—"

"Pardon me," gently interposed the visitor, "but it seems I know more about your office than you do. That is not the only door. There is another over there. Not behind that big iridescent rug. Your safe is behind that. Behind the reddish rug, just to the left of it."

Laing's scowl was wiped away into crass blankness.

"How do you know?" he rapped out. "Whose been blabbing or—or showing outsiders around here while I was away?"

"I don't know, I'm sure," answered the stranger. "But if you are wondering how *I* knew, the mystery is easily solved. Those two rugs are thin and limp. The window is open and there's a draught against them. The door-knob and the handle of the key under it are quite plainly outlined. As to the thick, short knob of the safe—"

"H'm!" grunted Laing. "You seem to use your eyes."

"I think that is what they were given to me for," gravely assented the other. "And I have had to make the best use of them. You see, I'm a thief."

Again, Ulrich Laing half-rose from his seat and again his fat hand crept toward the bell. Yet he scanned his guest's face sharply for trace of jest or mental aberration.

"Don't bother to ring," the stranger reassured him; "I am not here to rob you. And, by the way," he broke off, "let me give you a hint that will be of value to you: if you *must* carry your bill-folder in your upper left-hand vest pocket—a foolish place where every dip is certain to look first—don't raise your hand to it when you hear the word 'thief' mentioned."

Laing dropped his hand to the desk as though it burned him. But a reluctant grin began to twist his mouth-corners. This man amused him.

"I'm a thief," went on the visitor. "We'll call me Galvin Brenner, if you like. Partly because it happens to be my real name. I—"

"How did you get into my private office? Who let you in? The boy at the outer door—"

"Is still there, for all I know. He didn't see me. Because I didn't

want him to. I had to get to you, personally. A note would have done no good. You'd have thought I was a crank and refused to hear me."

"What do you want?"

"A job."

"Safe-cracking or merely second-story?" queried Laing, with the truly brilliant professional repartee which made him the sure-fire laugh-evoker of all his employees on such rare times as he deigned to unbend.

"Neither. I want a job in your store."

"My present staff robs me quite enough, I think," flashed Laing, with another inspiration of wit that showed him to be at his very best this morning. "They don't need any professional aid."

"You don't understand," protested Brenner, "and I'm wasting both your time and my own. Let me get down to business. I am a thief. A crook. I am thirty years old. For twelve years I have been living by my brains off the stupidity of gulls.

"I'm not a 'congenital criminal'—whatever that may mean. I have stolen because I was brought up to. I've steered clear of prison because I've had more sense—and maybe more luck—than most crooks. And now I'm turning honest."

"Why?" asked Laing, interested in spite of himself.

"Because there's nothing in the other game. Because it means a life of danger, of worry, of sleeping with one eye open, of such care and planning and foresight as no financier can employ. And in the end, even the best, luckiest crook clears up less than the average delicatessen dealer. By and by he gets too old to steal cleverly. Then he's nabbed or he goes to pieces and starves. There's nothing in it, I tell you. Half the work, along decent lines, would win a fortune. I'm through with it."

"That's why you're quitting?"

Brenner hesitated.

"That's one reason," he said sullenly. "The only one, I suppose, you'd believe. You'd laugh at me if I said I'd always envied men who weren't sick with fear, down in their hearts, every time some one touched them on the shoulder. Men who could look themselves in the glass, when they shave, and say: 'I may be down on my luck, but I'm clean. I'm *straight!*' Well, that's the way I want to be. It's the way I'm

going to be.

"I came into some money a little while ago. Not a fortune, but a few thousands. Clean money. From my aunt. Enough to keep me going while I look around, and while I am working my way up to a living wage. So I'm making the start."

"Very edifying!" yawned Laing, who found the latter half of the confession far less interesting than the first, and who was beginning to be bored. "But why tell all this to *me?*"

"To you? Why, I explained that. Because I'm coming to work for you."

"You seem quite certain."

"I am. You advertised in the Planet this morning for a rug salesman. I am a born salesman. I want the job. It's to your interest as much as to mine. I've no references. I could have had a dozen of them very neatly forged for me. But I want to start square. *Square.*"

"Quite so," agreed Laing, turning to the papers on his table. "But I'm sorry to say I've no opening for you. Good day."

Brenner's exaltation, bred of earnest, tense eagerness, fell from him at the rebuff. Once more he was the debonair man of the underworld.

"Hold on, Mr. Laing," said he. "You are going to hire me, I think. As much for your own sake as for mine. You want a salesman. I've told you, I'll make a good one. I want experience that will help me on my start at being honest. So I'll work harder than most beginners. I'm offering you, besides, all the skill and cleverness that have won me a place in a world where men are cleverer than in yours. I'm a bargain. Take me."

"This isn't bargain day in the Ulrich Laing Company."

"Listen to me!" urged the thief. "What did you expect to pay this salesman you advertised for?"

"I expected to start him on seventy-two dollars a month, raising him as he proved worth while and then giving him a commission and salary. That is our custom. But—"

"Good. Well, I'll start on seventy-two dollars, and stay at that till you think I'm worth a raise."

"I wasn't going to pay seventy-two dollars to a greenhorn. I advertised for a man who knew rugs."

"That's easily fixed. Tell me once the name of a rug and show me

the rug, and I'll guarantee never to forget either its name or its make. Inside of a week I'll know your stock backward. Inside of a *day*. Try me."

Laing, nettled at the fellow's calm assurance, thrust out a finger toward one of the floor rugs and growled an Oriental name. In almost the same breath he indicated a wall rug and creaked out a title chiefly made up of guttural consonants.

A third and fourth he designated, naming each and a fifth.

Then he turned sneeringly to Brenner.

"There!" he announced. "I've 'told you once' the names of the rugs and shown them to you. You say you'll guarantee never to forget. Let me hear you point out and name three out of the five I've just shown you."

"Whew!" laughed Brenner, "I had no idea there were so many outlandish names in the world. I've heard of Bokharas and Shervans and Khorassans and Daghestans and a few other 'ans,' but these are new ones on me."

"Stumped, eh?"

"Stumped? Not noticeably. Let me see."

Methodically he touched every rug in turn that Laing had pointed out, and at each touch he named that especial rug correctly. It was a feat of memory and of observation that caused Laing's little eyes to open wide.

"You know rugs," he accused.

"I know these five. Are there more kinds?"

Laing eyed him long and thoughtfully.

"If you *do* know rugs," he said at last, "so much the better. If you don't, a trained memory like yours would master the outer details of the business in no time. So you'd be willing to start at seventy-two dollars?"

"Yes."

"How would you live while you're learning to make good? "

"I've told you I received a little legacy lately."

"Oh, yes. From your uncle. I remember."

"No. From my aunt."

"And you've really been a crook for fifteen years?"

Again Brenner laughed; pleasantly, heartily.

"Mr. Laing," said he, "twelve years, I said. If you're trying to trip me up in my story, as you seem to be, you're wasting time. Why, man, don't you suppose if I chose to lie, a memory like mine could master every point in my lie; so that I couldn't be cornered?

"But it's nothing to me whether you believe me or not. I want a chance to be honest and make good. I can get money, all sorts of money. But I want *honest* money. I'll work for you as no other employee will. I want a chance."

"So you said."

"It's harder to turn honest than you think. To start out without references, with the Brand of the Crook on you. To know your boss will always doubt you and that if anything is missing from the store during the next ten years you'll be suspected. I'm ready to fight down all those obstacles. Give me a chance."

"To learn the value of my goods and the combination of my safe and how to get into my store at night?"

"Yes. If you choose to put it that way. As to getting into your store, that would be child's play. I've never seen your safe, except through that rug hanging over it. But I'll engage to open it in four minutes. As to stealing your goods, I can do that as easily 'from the outside' as in your employ. I repeat, I'm a bargain."

"Why did you pick out my advertisement rather than any other?"

"Because you were pointed out to me once, in the Knickerbocker bar. I size up faces pretty easily. It is part of my trade."

"And you sized up mine?"

"As the sort of man who would—understand the crook temperament. As the sort of man who is honest for revenue only. The man who isn't above taking a good bargain if that bargain happens to be marked 'crooked.' That's the sort of bargain *I* am. It's up to you."

There was a pause, while Laing slowly digested Brenner's words and did some rather rapid thinking.

"When can you come to work?" asked the rug king at last.

"I'm here now," replied Galvin Brenner. "Mr. Laing, you and I are going to get on swimmingly. But I've a hunch that things will happen."

CHAPTER II.

For Sale: Forty Ali Babas.

WITHIN three days Galvin Brenner had mastered details of the rug business that the average beginner could not have hoped to grasp in as many months.

The "price code" he had learned and could read as easily as the plainest figures, after half an hour of study.

The names and textures of rugs that he had once seen remained photographed indelibly in his memory.

Laing's reluctant admiration for his new salesman grew apace. The more so when, on the second day, Brenner quietly lifted two fingers as a countrified customer was leaving the store.

The stranger, with a lightning-quick gesture, dropped two small but costly rugs from under his coat and fled.

On the third morning, as on the second, Brenner was the first salesman to enter the store; just as the porter was laying down the rugs and putting the place to rights. Full of zeal at his new trade, Brenner helped the porter arrange stock, and waited, with a truly bewitching grace, on an old lady who had dropped in on her way to an out-of-town train.

Presently a second porter came in with a big bundle of rugs that had just arrived from the custom house.

Brenner fell upon them, cut their binding cord and spread them out in one corner of the outer shop to await Mr. Laing's arrival.

They were not large nor, to his mind, especially prepossessing. Nor were they of any of the designs or fabrics to which he had accustomed himself during the past two days.

There were forty of them. And on the cord that bound them, as well as on the outermost rug of the bundle, were scrawled two tagged letters. So badly were the letters printed that Brenner was forced to examine them for a moment or two before he could decipher them as "M. P."

At once he understood.

The letters represented the retail code price. Most stores have such

ciphers; each letter representing a numeral; the whole cipher forming a ten-letter word or phrase whose first letter corresponds with the number "1" and the last with "0."

The Ulrich Laing Company's cipher was "Make Profit." Thus, as a single glance showed Brenner, "M. P." stood for "15." And as no decimal marks were apparent, the retail code price of the rugs was, of course, fifteen dollars.

Scarcely had he gleaned this bit of information when the head salesman called up on the telephone to say he was ill with grippe and could not come down to work that day. The second clerk lived somewhere in New Jersey and was prone to missing trains. He, too, had not yet arrived. The third salesman—as always on a morning when consignments from the East were due—was down at the Custom House.

Mr. Laing was also unaccountably late. And Brenner realized suddenly, with a thrill of real pride, that he himself chanced to be the only salesman on duty. After two days of employment he temporarily represented the entire selling force of the great rug-house of Ulrich Laing. On his shoulders rested full responsibility.

Meantime, customers were beginning to drop in. It was the "first flight" of early shoppers. An elderly man was among the earliest. Drifting idly through the store he chanced to note the forty new rugs, some rolled, some flat, in their corner of the front show-room.

He stooped, picked up one of them; held it to the light, felt its texture and shook it slowly to catch a view of the sheen along its surface.

"What rugs are these?" he asked, indicating the one in his hand and the thirty-nine other new arrivals.

Brenner had been expecting such a question. And his answer was ready.

While he had a parrot memory for the name and good points of every rug that had been described to him during the past two days, yet this consignment seemed to contain no rugs of the kind he had been shown. Nor had any invoice or bill of lading accompanied the bundle. That was doubtless in the pocket of the clerk who piloted the forty rugs through the custom house.

Wherefore, Galvin Brenner resolved to bluff.

He dared not classify these rugs under any of the names he had learned, lest the buyer might be familiar with such varieties. And as he cast about for an Oriental name, the new consignment's number, forty, awoke in him a train of association.

"I asked what rugs these are," repeated the customer a little impatiently.

"These?" echoed Brenner. "Oh, these are the famous Ali Baba weave. We are introducing them into America. You will see from the—"

"How much is this one?"

"They are all fifteen dollars apiece. Please don't laugh at the absurdly low price for such treasures. As I said, we are introducing them here. And so we are letting the first lot go out at a shameful sacrifice. A month from now, one hundred dollars wouldn't buy a rug like this. You will note that the weave—"

"I'll take this. And this. And that one over there."

"You are wise, sir, to get in on the ground floor. A month from now—By the way, shall we add one more rug and make it an even sixty dollars? That—"

"Yes."

"And—"

"Those four will be enough for the present. Have them wrapped up and phone for a taxi. I will take them with me."

Before the elderly man had finished counting out his money, a woman who had entered the store wandered over to see what her fellow shopper had bought. Noticing that he had selected four rugs from an especial collection, she too became absorbed in Ali Babas.

And ten minutes later she left with two of them.

Her interest in them attracted two other early customers. And so on for the next two hours, at the end of which time twelve of the Ali Babas had been sold.

They were sent to the delivery department with orders to distribute them on the first trip.

Then the belated New Jersey salesman came in and Brenner was relegated to his proper place in the rear of the store.

But he was in a glow. He had made good. The "rug king" was certain to be pleased.

Forty Ali Babas and a Thief

"Who was on duty here when the store opened?" demanded Ulrich Laing as he hurried in a few minutes later. "You?"

"I certainly was. And I sold—"

"I went down to the Custom House myself this morning to handle a special consignment of rugs and bring them up here in person. The boat docked an hour before schedule time. And when I got there I found Caton had already sent them up. They come all right? Where—"

"Yes. All forty of them. A couple of hours ago. But—"

"Good. I was afraid they might—"

"But they're not all here *now*, by a long shot."

"What do you mean?"

"I mean, Mr. Laing, that I sold no less than twelve of those forty rugs in two hours!"

He looked expectantly at his employer, ready to enjoy the latter's amaze at such quick work by a greenhorn.

And the amazement he looked for was assuredly visible. Indeed, it was writ large all over Ulrich Laing's wide face, turning the ruddy visage an ashy gray and making the little eyes pop out like a lobster's.

"You—sold—you sold—" babbled Laing thickly.

"Twelve in two hours. They went like gold bricks. They went so fast I wished I dared run up their price from fifteen dollars to—"

"*Fifteen dollars!*" croaked Laing, a queer paralysis holding him moveless and all but dumb.

"Yes. That was the retail code price—'M. P.'—fifteen dollars. And if Parker hadn't come in to take charge, I believe I'd have the whole forty sold by now. Better put me in the front of the store, Mr. Laing. I told you I was a born salesman. I—"

"You're a born criminal idiot!" bellowed Laing, suddenly finding his voice and his motive power. "You've wrecked us! Where are the rest of those forty rugs?"

"Over there. What's wrong?"

But Laing had torn away and was actually galloping across to where the twelve unsold items of the "Ali Baba" consignment were lying. He threw himself upon the relics, sorting, examining, muttering, his hands palsied, his breath coming in short gasps.

As he reached the last of the twelve, Brenner standing bewilderedly over him, Laing threw up both arms and cried in stark horror:

"Gone! *Gone!* Good Lord! *Gone!*"

"What?" began Brenner.

But blindly Ulrich Laing lurched away and rushed into his private office, slamming and locking the door behind him.

CHAPTER III.

A Strange Quest.

FOR a full half-hour Brenner stood mooning around the shop, wondering mightily what had happened—and why.

He realized he had made a mistake. Presumably a big one, judging from the usually self-contained Laing's almost babyish emotion. But what was the blunder? His suspense came to an end at last. Laing's errand boy hurried into the front store with a summons for the delinquent to come immediately to the private office.

Brenner obeyed, bracing himself disgustedly for a further exhibition of horror on the part of the rug king.

To his surprise and relief, he found Laing seated calmly at his table-desk in the rug-lined office, bearing no sign whatever of his recent distress. Brenner found it in his heart to admire the man's powers of restraint.

"Sit down, Brenner," said Laing, indicating the only other chair that was not rug-strewn.

Brenner seated himself, alertly waiting for the next move.

"Brenner," continued Laing in the same even voice, "you sold twelve rugs this morning. You sold them at fifteen dollars each. You seem to expect me to commend your zeal. My only excuse for not doing so is that each of those rugs was worth more than one thousand dollars."

"No!" gasped Brenner.

"That may account," resumed Laing, "for the ease with which you were able to get rid of them for fifteen dollars apiece. The merest tyro among our customers could see what wonderful value he was getting for his money."

"But the code price—the 'M. P.' on each?"

"That was not a code price. It was an Arabic sign. Looking at it upside down, I suppose, it was barely possible that an ignorant man might have mistaken the symbol for these two letters. You evidently did."

"Mr. Laing," said Brenner abruptly, "I've played the fool. And, like most fools, I've harmed some one else instead of myself. If I had twelve thousand dollars, or anywhere near that sum, I'd pay it over to you to square things. But I haven't. My legacy was only four thousand nine hundred dollars. I've got most of it left. Of course, I'll transfer that to you. And pay up as much of the rest as I can, from time to time."

"I suppose one good haul from a safe-cracking job would do it?" sneered Laing.

Brenner flushed slightly under his tanned skin.

"I'm afraid I can't help you that way, Mr. Laing," he said stiffly. "When I said I had dropped the old game, I meant it. Henceforth I play square. If there's any honest way I can get the money for you—"

"There's a way you can get the rugs back for me. At least, I think there may be. That is why I sent for you just now, instead of discharging you out of hand. Are you sincere in your wish to atone for this gross and costly blunder of yours?"

"Try me," said Brenner, steadily.

"Good. You say you were a crook for twelve years. Well, here is a chance to put your predatory talents to use in a good cause. Steal back those rugs for me."

"Steal?"

"Oh, call it by any name you like. *Get* them. They are mine. They were sold under a misapprehension."

"But—"

"If your new-born conscience bothers you, you can leave the cost price in place of them when you take them. If I sent to the purchasers and asked them to sell back for fifteen dollars what is worth more than a thousand, they would laugh in my face. Will you do it?"

Brenner walked to the window and stood there, his hands behind him, looking out. Long he stood there, motionless, his back to Laing. And the rug king eyed him as tensely as might a speculator the ticker whose next purr will mean fortune or failure.

At length Brenner turned back into the room. At sight of his face Laing caught a breath of relief.

For Brenner's eyes were aglow with the light that was, perhaps, resolution, perhaps mischief, perhaps both. Possibly a feminine novelist might have described it as "the joy of battle."

"You're on," he said briefly.

"You'll do it?"

"I'll get you as many of those rugs as I can lay hands on."

"And for each you bring me," chimed in Laing, "I'll give you—"

"You'll give me nothing," contradicted Brenner. "And it'll be my own money I leave in their place."

"Good!" assented Laing, with genial patronage. "That's the way I like to hear a man talk. I got the list of addresses for you. Here it is."

"You must have been pretty sure of my consenting to steal them back."

"Brenner, my boy," laughed Laing, "I owe most of my success to being able to size up men; and some of the rest of it to my habit of trying to sop up spilled milk instead of crying over it."

"And I'm to do the sopping for you? All right. Each rug I get I'll bring to you at once. Good-by."

CHAPTER IV.

Underground Work.

UNWONTEDLY early each morning thereafter Ulrich Laing reached his office. Daily he expected to find Brenner awaiting him there with one of the lost rugs.

But days passed, and with them no Brenner.

The thief was busy night and day. He knew it was not enough to have the addresses of the rugs' present owners. He could scarce march into the houses of such people, locate and snatch up a rug, and depart unchallenged.

There must be no danger of failure nor of capture. That would at once end his campaign of restoration.

Wherefore, he laid his plans as carefully and as cunningly as though he were arranging the theft of the British crown jewels.

By devious courses, he traced half a dozen of the rugs; learned the nature and occupants of the abodes in which each was domiciled, and, as far as possible, the characters and weaknesses of the possessors themselves.

More than once during his researches, he called for help from his old comrades of the underworld, and for that help he paid well.

More than once he found himself—as canvasser, gas inspector, telephone lineman, or delivery man—in the very presence of one of the coveted rugs. At last his line of advance was ready, and he prepared to angle for the first half-dozen of the "Ali Babas."

After that, a new campaign could be mapped out for the hardest part of all—the tracing of the rugs that had been carried from the store by hand instead of by delivery.

Mr. Morrie Cauler had just reopened his popular and well-established place of business on a side street just north of Forty-Second Street and west of Broadway.

Mr. Cauler's establishment had suffered a temporary eclipse, due to an overinterest on the part of the local district attorney's office.

He had long since persuaded the precinct police captain that his house was a good one to overlook. And this persuasion had been backed by a politician of high repute and by a monthly subscription to an unlisted civic fund.

But the district attorney's men, unjustly distrusting police aid, had one night descended without warning and with a hydraulic jack, upon the Cauler palace of mischance; had cruelly refused to believe that certain perfectly innocent contraptions on view there were other than roulette wheels and faro layouts, and had not only taken certain prisoners (on "John Dealer" and "James Wheelman" warrants) but had wrecked the whole establishment.

Thus, when a gentler and more amenable district attorney came into office and Cauler was enabled to open once more for business, the house needed thorough refurnishing.

After which a house-warming ensued.

At this function Mr. Cauler was pleased to see his old acquain-

tance, Galvin Brenner.

There had been disquieting rumors that Brenner had "gone good." And Cauler was glad that the suspected man should clear his bad name by public reappearance at this wholesale reunion of the underworld. Also that Brenner should take so keen and critical an interest in the new furnishings. It was a pleasure to see his absorption in the costly rugs and draperies.

A hired decorator had done the job, and had charged for it the gilt-edged price that the underworld was always taxed for its garish luxuries. The admiration of a man like Brenner went far to reconcile Cauler to the decorator's bill.

In fact, Brenner could not keep his eyes off the sumptuous display long enough to patronize the tables to any profitable extent. A whirl or two of the wheel, five minutes at the faro layout—and off he would be on another delighted inspection of the room.

The hour grew late and play ran high. Men in evening clothes—known habitues of the place and, as such, admitted by the "wicket man" began to fill the gaudy rooms—drifting in from clubs, theaters, and dances.

And before the advent of these more profitable customers, the underworld gradually effaced itself.

But Brenner stayed on. He was no longer interested in the habiliments of the place, but in one roulette wheel. Here he played steadily, but without system, staking very small sums on the colors and on the *"pair et impair"* and seldom varying in fortune.

An observer would have scored him as a piker or as lacking interest in the game. But at such places there are few observers of men whose play is small and conservative.

A "plunger" entered. He began to play heavily. All eyes in that part of the room, except those of the actual players, were on him. Brenner strolled over to the buffet.

His cigarette fell on a small rug that lay there.

He picked up the rug with no effort at concealment and began to brush off the ashes he had spilled on it. Then, his back to the rest, and facing the buffet, he folded the rug and slipped it under his coat. He did it unconcernedly.

No one noted. All eyes were still on the game or on the plunger.

A minute later, Brenner was gone. So was the rug. On the buffet corner lay three five-dollar bills twisted into a spill.

Down the thick carpeted stairs Brenner sped. Along the hall toward the guarded front door. And as he went he shed the cheap waistcoat he wore.

In its place, beneath his close-buttoning business coat, he wrapped around his chest and waist the rug. The rug for whose acquisition he had spoiled Morrie Cauler's house-warming.

Past the lookout he hurried and laid his hand on the doorknob.

As he did so there was a sudden crash. The door flew inward, almost knocking him down, and a cataract of blue-clad men gushed into the hallway.

CHAPTER V.

Flight!

A NEW police captain had been slated for the precinct which was honored by the presence of Mr. Morrie Cauler's temple of chance.

He had come on duty that afternoon, instead of the following morning, as had been originally planned.

He was a reformer—until the right people in the district could have time to argue away his reform ideas. And a spectacular raid, at the outset, seemed the quickest way to set such arguments in motion.

Hence the descent upon Cauler.

The customary warning had not been sent. The police had massed quietly.

The hydraulic jack had been applied with so little noise that even the lookout had not time to spread the alarm before the door was burst in.

Galvin Brenner gathered as many of the foregoing facts as were needful to his personal uses in a smaller fraction of a second than any three hundred dollar stop-watch has yet learned to indicate.

His body working as quickly as his mind, he leaped back behind the in-flying door, and crouched there for an instant while the bulk of the raiders surged into the house.

Then, bending low, he darted out, ducked under the upflung arm of a policeman in the vestibule, dodged a second unprepared bluecoat at the top of the steps, cleared the nine brownstone steps in one flying leap and—landed in the arms of a patrolman at the bottom.

The impact knocked his captor off his balance.

Wriggling like an eel, Brenner twisted himself free before the policeman could renew his grip, and made off at a "hundred-yard" clip toward the North River.

Ordinarily, so old a denizen of the underworld as Galvin Brenner would not have exerted himself in the very least to avoid capture in a gambling-house raid. For he knew that mere patrons of such places usually suffer no worse fate than a temporary inconvenience of appearing before a magistrate, answering to the time-honored cognomen of "John Smith," and then escaping with a perfunctory scolding from the bench.

But, just now, Brenner could not afford to he caught. At the station house he would have a hard time explaining how he came to be wearing a Persian rug instead of a vest. Cauler would recognize the rug. And not only would Brenner lose forever his standing in the underworld, but—what was of infinitely more import—he would lose the rug as well.

Wherefore he ran. And, because he ran, two policemen gave chase.

And one of the two, being new to the force and to the possession of firearms, drew his pistol and fired.

The bullet passed between Galvin's arm and his ribs, scratching viciously through the side of his coat in its whizzing flight.

The hour was very late, the side street dark. Not a soul was on the sidewalk ahead of Brenner as he raced toward Ninth Avenue.

His heels were light, and he was gaining slowly on the two panting bluecoats, one of whom, without checking his pace, smote every few moments on the pavement with his night-stick.

That signal and the pistol-shot, Brenner knew, were certain to bring every policeman on beat in that section of Ninth Avenue on the run to head him off. There was no hope of gaining the docks.

Even as he realized this, the thing he had dreaded happened. Under the glare of electric light that marked the Clark street's egress into Ninth Avenue, a third policeman appeared.

The fugitive was neatly pocketed.

Scarce slacking his pace he dashed into the areaway of an apartment

house.

He opened the area door by smashing the glass and turning the key on the inside. Then he darted back into the ash cupboard under the front steps and concealed himself.

In an instant the two policemen were in the areaway. Seeing the broken glass and open door they rushed into the basement hall, colliding in the dark with a sleepy janitor aroused by the racket.

And in the ensuing scrimmage Galvin Brenner calmly stepped out of the ash bin and regained the street and safety.

Ulrich Laing reached his store next morning to find Brenner awaiting him. The emissary followed Laing into the inner office and spread out on the desk a somewhat dusty rug.

"I brushed it as well as I could," he explained, as he finished the story of the night's events. "But the area ash bin was the only safe place to hide in."

Laing was not observing the ashes, but a faint groove that showed on the rug's under surface. Brenner followed his glance.

"I hope that scratch won't injure the rug's value," said he. "It's where the cop's bullet grazed. My coat got it much worse. See?"

"Brenner," remarked Laing after a thought-laden silence, "you're something of a man. I think I like you. Sit down and have a smoke while you tell me more about the chase."

"Thanks," refused Brenner, "but I haven't time to smoke or to brag. There are still eleven rugs to get. I must work faster if I don't want to make a life job of my hunt. Good-by. I'm off for the next."

CHAPTER VI.

Sanctuary!

FATHER AMBROSE CURRAN sat in his parish house study.

House and appointments were new and were adjuncts to the lately built Church of St. Festus, which reared its spire in the heart of an upper East Side slum as a rallying-point in its never-ending battle

with the sin and sorrow and poverty that so tightly hemmed it in.

The little parish house had been furnished by loving and loyal hands.

Yet as he looked about, for the hundredth time, at its simple luxury, Father Curran wished once more that his living and working quarters might have represented less outlay and that he might have had the spending of the price-difference for his adored poor.

Then scolding himself roundly for his own ingratitude, the priest bent once more to the task of preparing his monthly parish reports.

But they were doomed to delay this afternoon. Within a single half-hour he was interrupted by two whining appeals for money aid; by a wife who wanted his prayers and his counsel for a drinking husband; by a girl who was soliciting clerical advertisements for a Sunday newspaper, and by a man who had come to make a thank-offering to the church.

This last-named caller came on business of such rarity and of so wholesome a nature that Father Curran felt his own battered faith in human nature reviving.

"I won't take more than a moment of your busy time, father," began this thank-offering man in a brisk, businesslike voice, as he set down the suit-case he carried and accepted the chair tendered him.

"Here's my case: I have had a little stroke of luck. And I'd like to donate a percentage of it to your poor. Will you attend to its distribution for me, in any way you see fit? I shall be obliged to you. The sum I'm giving is small. Only fifteen dollars. I wish it were bigger. Here it is."

He laid a ten-dollar bill and a five on the desk and rose to his feet to go.

"I thank you most heartily," said Father Curran. "I wish more men when they have what you call 'a little stroke of luck' would remember our unfortunates in this way—"

He broke off in dismay. The caller, while extending his hand to meet the priest's in farewell, had suddenly cried out and collapsed into his chair.

"You are ill?" exclaimed Father Curran in dire concern. "You are suffering? Let me telephone for—"

"No!" gasped the stricken man. "A touch of—of vertigo. I often—

often—Drink of water, please—I—"

The priest hastened from the room before the stammering appeal was completed. Quickly he came back with a glass of cold water which he held to the visitor's twitching lips.

At a draft the young man emptied the glass, then sighed and opened his eyes wider. After which he rose somewhat shakily to his feet.

"Thank you," he murmured. "I'm—I'm all right again now. I often have these turns. There's nothing serious about them. And they're over in a few minutes. I'm sorry to have bothered you so."

As he spoke he stooped and picked up his suit-case.

"Hold on!" urged Father Curran, "you are surely not well enough yet to go out. Lie down over there on my couch for a while. I'll have my housekeeper make you some strong coffee."

"No, thanks," returned the other, "I'm all right. Good day."

"But let me go with you as far as your home," insisted the priest. "You may have another attack and—"

"It isn't necessary," growled the visitor ungraciously. "I'm well again. Besides, you're busy."

"Oh, I can spare time easily for such a trifling service as that," exclaimed Father Curran, with a guilty look at his work-piled desk. "I'll get my hat and—"

"I'd rather be alone, thanks. I'm quite recovered. Good-by."

The stranger turned abruptly on his heel and, suit-case in hand, cut short further argument by striding bruskly from the room and from the house.

"What an odd man!" commented Father Curran, going back to his desk. "Almost rude, in spite of being so generous."

He set himself to work again, but, even as he sifted out statistics and filed appeals, his mind reverted to his late guest.

"A thank-offering," he mused. "And in money! How much wiser than to spend it on furnishings that I've no right to sell for people who need help! Yes, the desk must be worth eighty dollars. And then that fancy rug—Why, bless my soul, where *is* the rug?"

He stared blankly at one equally blank space on the floor in front of the desk. Then he looked in bewildered fashion about the floor, on the chance that his housekeeper might have placed the rug elsewhere

in the room.

And his wandering gaze at last fell on a figure that was just entering the study doorway. It was his recent visitor, the thank-offering man.

At sight of him Farther Curran quite forgot the mystery of the vanished rug.

"You were feeling worse," he cried, "and so you came back! You did right. Lie down there, and I'll telephone for our own doctor. It's the hot weather, probably. But he'll have you all right in no time. He's a splendid doctor."

"I am not sick," answered the visitor, in a curiously constrained voice, like that of a scared child that admits a grievous fault.

"But—" began the priest.

"Father Curran," blurted the stranger, flinging open his suitcase as he spoke, "here is your rug. I thought I could go through with this job. But I can't. I draw the line at cheating the Church. Send for the police, if you like."

CHAPTER VII.

Confession.

FATHER AMBROSE CURRAN looked long and silently at the thief. And as he looked he read the face of the man before him as lesser souls might read a printed page.

Into his mild eyes dawned a light that transformed and almost glorified them. Then—

"Sit down, my son," he said gently. "It seems that you and I have much to say to each other. It is tiring to stand when one has just been ill. Sit down."

"I was not ill," said Brenner sullenly, "it was part of the dirty trick I played you. I pretended to be sick and asked for water to get you out of the room while I stole this rug. I lied to you. Even about the 'thank-offering.' I lied to a man who trusted me. The first man who ever trusted me.

"And I robbed you while you were trying to do me a kindness. I

suppose," he finished with almost impersonal disgust, "I suppose I've dropped just about as low as a thief can."

"You are not a thief," gravely corrected the priest. "So far as I am concerned you are honest. If sudden temptation has made you take what was not yours, you just have atoned by restitution and by confession and by offer to endure punishment for your faults. You stand before me—absolved!

"But," he went on presently, "why should you have taken the rug? If booty was your object there are costlier things here. In this drawer there is money. And—if you are a thief—why did you bring me money as a thief? If it is part of a stolen sum," he broke off sternly, "I warn you I will not accept—"

"No," answered Brenner, "it was not."

"You saw me put your fifteen dollars in the drawer," continued the bewildered priest, "and you must have seen there was more money there. Why did you not take that as well as the rug?"

"I do not need money. I need the rug. I cannot explain. And I am not a crank. Nor," Brenner continued, "in the sense you use the word, am I a thief any longer."

"I do not understand," replied the priest, "I do not understand any of it. But this I do know: you are a penitent man—a soul in pain—at heart a man who longs to be good. Since you wish this rug, take it. It is yours."

"No!"

"You have already paid me its probable value in that supposed 'thank-offering.' Take it. It is yours, by my free gift. A man could not so lower himself for anything as you have done for this rug, unless behind it all were some powerful motive. I do not ask what that motive is. If you were wrong in your impulse, you have proved your repentance. Take the rug."

"Let me pay you—"

"You have already paid. In more than money. Listen!" Father Curran's eyes sparkled with sudden laughter. "I will tell you a secret. Even when you came back, I was wishing my furnishings here could have been simpler and the money they cost could be put to uses that would make me happier.

"It was an ungrateful—an unworthy wish. But you have made part

of it come true. Now we have both confessed.

"I can see you are anxious to be gone. And I have work to do. Good-by. And—if ever I can help you, remember the door of God's house stands always open."

At the nearest post-office sub-station Brenner bought a hundred dollar money order, signing a fictitious name to the application blank. And he mailed it to Father Curran.

"He'll have trouble refusing *that* installment on my debt," thought Brenner as he hurried down-town toward the great rug-emporium.

He arrived just at closing time and entered the private office as Ulrich Laing was climbing into his street coat.

Without a word Brenner spread out the rug on the desk.

Laing, as before, shot a keen glance at the rug; then frowned slightly, as though in disappointment. But instantly his face cleared.

"Come, come!" he exclaimed, ponderously genial, "this *is* progress. Two in one day. At that rate we'll have the lot of them back inside of a week. Let's hear the story of the second adventure."

He leaned back in his chair, an expectant smile overspreading his puffy, florid face.

"There's no story," said Brenner curtly. "At least—none that you could understand. And if there were, I've no time to tell it. I've a busy night before me."

CHAPTER VIII.

A Queer Find.

VAN CLEEK DUYCK went home. Chiefly for the time-honored reason that there seemed to be no other place to go.

He had run out to the Arareek Country Club for the night, to be on hand at a strictly illegal prize-fight that a group of the club members were planning to engineer in a near-by barn at dawn on the following day.

It was to be an informal and old-fashioned bout, such as they had read of the "Corinthian bloods" attending in the days of George

IV. Each fighter had his clique of frenzied backers among the club members. The battle was to be the most exclusive on record. Barely fifty spectators, and that fifty representing as many millions.

The whole thing had been one of the happy inspirations of Van Cleek Duyck's fertile brain. And it had been loudly acclaimed. In fact it had been just a trifle too loudly acclaimed. So loudly indeed that it had reached the straining ears of Sheriff Flick of Arareek County.

The sheriff had been plenteously blackballed by the ultra-close Arareek Country Club. And now, by way of jocund repartee, he proceeded at the eleventh hour to arrest both fighters and to hold them, temporarily, without bail as "disorderly characters and menaces to the peace of Arareek County in the State of New York."

The sad news had confronted Van Cleek Duyck on his arrival at the club that evening. And as his fellow members seemed inclined to blame him for the fiasco, he did not enjoy his stay there.

After various libations he decided that he hated everybody, and he came back to town on the 10.50 train.

He did not care to be seen at any club or restaurant. For, at such a place, some fool of his acquaintance was certain to ask questions about the fight. And he did not want to do any more explaining just then.

It was too late to go to a show or to call anywhere. So, against every precedent in his short but event-strewn career, Van Cleek Duyck actually went to his own home at the unheard of hour of 11.45 P.M.

Such a thing had not happened in a year. He had given his valet the evening off. His three Jap house-servants, relying on their employer's regular custom of returning homeward in conjunction with the morning papers, had fared forth on a night of celestial recreation at the Nippon Club.

Wherefore, the early-arriving Van Cleek Duyck was hazily pained to find his "house left unto him desolate."

He fortified himself with a comforter or two at the sideboard; then roamed lazily upward toward his bedroom; singing plaintively, off key, as he went.

At the door of his room he felt for the electric key; he turned it and set aglow the shaded light clusters on three walls. He was sober—to a modified degree—but he was very unhappy.

He had been so happy, no later than last night! He remembered how he had sung a blithe roundelay as he came up-stairs then— conquering the writhing banisters and the wobbly steps. He recalled how droll had been the antics of the rug just within his bedroom doorway. It had jumped up and embraced him around the ankles; playfully trying to throw him.

Even that merry little door rug, apparently, lacked the heart to rise and frolic with him. Poor little rug!

And—say, where *was* that romp-loving rug? Who had dared move it from its fall-inducing resting place?

Maybe it had crawled under the bed. He would look.

Yes, it was altogether likely the poor, ill-treated rug had crawled under the bed; since there was no other hiding place so accessible in all the room.

Mr. Van Cleek Duyck went ponderously on all fours and reached a long, groping arm beneath the bed's white side lattice.

His reaching fingers promptly found and triumphantly closed around—a man's ankle.

CHAPTER IX.

For High Stakes.

TO look under his bed for a rug and to find, instead, a fellow man seemed to Van Cleek Duyck the most deliciously mirth-provoking episode in all his experience.

His gloom was swept away by a gust of overjoyous laughter. Releasing the squirming ankle, he collapsed into a sitting posture on the floor and laughed until the room rang with his merriment.

And as he sat thus, the man under the bed began slowly to emerge.

Duyck, speechless, helpless from laughter, sat, goggle-eyed and open-mouthed, watching the gradual appearance of a pair of hands, then a head, then broad shoulders.

He had pictured mentally—so far as his present mentality could picture anything—a bullet-headed, unshaven ruffian with bristling

black jowl, a soiled handkerchief about his neck, and a jimmy and a dark lantern in either hand.

Instead, his uninvited guest had a clean, strong face, well-cut clothes, and in place of jimmy or lantern—he drew from under the bed after him an Oriental rug.

"This belongs to you, I think?" suavely observed the intruder as he rose, brushing off the knees and elbows of his suit. "I commend your servants or your housekeeper. I've seldom found the floor under any bed so clean."

"Wh—what were you doing under there?" demanded Duyck weakly, the laugh-spasm almost clearing his brain. "And what did you take the rug there for? It—it doesn't make sense."

"Oh, yes, it does," Brenner reassured him. "It's plain as day, when you've got the diagram. It's usually the comic paper burglar that hides under the bed. But, at a pinch, it's a hiding-place not to be despised."

"You're—you're a burglar? "

"Do I look like a war-scare? Who but a burglar would be hiding under your bed at this time of night? I was after this rug."

He folded it neatly and tucked it under his left arm.

But Duyck, still sitting cross-legged on the floor, wagged a reproving forefinger at him.

"'Twon't work, old scout!" admonished the sitter. "'Twon't work. Never heard a clumshier lie in all my life. Came up here to look for a cheap rug, and skipped all the perf'ly good silver in the dining-room? No, no! Too bald. Too shiny. Won't work. 'Fraid you're only a poor, measly honest man. Get out!"

"Gladly," assented Brenner. "There's only one more thing to do before I go. Here."

From his pocket he drew a five-dollar bill folded around a ten-dollar gold piece.

"What's that for?" queried the puzzled Duyck.

"To pay for the rug, of course. Since you've so mercilessly exposed me as an honest man, I'll have to live up to the part. Here."

He dropped the money into one of Duyck's feebly gesticulating palms.

"Hold on!" commanded Duyck with awful sternness. "What'cher take me for? I'm no bally rug-dealer. That rug isn't for sale, either.

And, besides, it's most likely worth a lot more than what you're trying to pay me for it. My man got it for me when I burned a cigarette-hole through another one and—"

"And he paid fifteen dollars for it at Ulrich Laing's. What he taxed you for it I don't know. But there's the fifteen. Good-by."

"I'm not selling!" solemnly retorted Duyck. "I'm holding for a rise. What'cher want the rug for, anyhow? What'cher doing in my house at all?"

"I'm buying rugs, as I told you. And, having bought, I'm going."

Brenner took a step toward the door; but Duyck caught him by the trousers leg.

"You stop where you are," ordered the clubman, "or I'll lick you."

"My little friend," soothed Brenner, making no effort to escape, "I want this rug. I have only to land on your jaw to put you out of business while I make a getaway. Don't force me to. If the price isn't enough—"

"Now, that's a fair offer!" declared Duyck, scrambling to his feet. "Come on up-stairs to the gym. We'll put on the gloves. If you can put me out, the rug's yours. If you can't, why—it isn't. Fair sporting offer. Come on up."

Brenner mentally contrasted his own bulk and clean, athletic strength with the thin-chested, swaying figure before him.

"I'm afraid you are too formidable a boxer for me," he replied. "You're 'way above my class."

"Quite right!" beamed Duyck, highly pleased. "Sensible man to avoid a licking. Play you a poker hand for the rug. One cold hand."

Brenner hesitated.

Common sense told him to rap the half drunken fellow over the head, or to gag and tie him up, and to walk off in safety with the rug. But it irked him to do violence to a man so palpably helpless. It was like snatching a toy from a crying child.

In poker, luck is with the drunk as fully as with the sober. And something about Duyck's innate sportsmanship appealed to the plunderer.

"One poker hand," repeated his host. "One cold poker hand!"

He shuffled to a table and drew out a deck of cards encased in a red silk case. Riffling the cards with a rare skill for one whose fingers were

so unsteady, he offered them to Brenner to cut.

Brenner merely tapped the deck with his finger-tips. And, with a nod of appreciation, Duyck proceeded to deal two hands—face upward.

He dealt with a lightning speed and accuracy, betokening years of instinct and skill beneath momentary haziness.

Not until he had dealt the tenth card did he glance at his own hand, lying scattered on the little table before him. And by that time Brenner's face could have told him the story of the deal.

Duyck had two pair—sevens and tens. Brenner's hand could boast but a pair of fives.

"You win!" philosophically observed the visitor.

CHAPTER X.

From Frying-Pan to Fire.

BLINKING, Duyck peered across at Brenner and studied his face with wavering intensity. But the latter showed no hint of chagrin. Not a muscle betrayed a sense of loss nor of defeat.

"Good!" approved Van Cleek Duyck with tipsy solemnity. "I said you weren't a burglar. And I said—or I'd have said it if I'd thought to—that you've got good blood. And now I think I'll join myself in a drink to celebrate. Have one?"

"No, thanks."

"No? You're wise," remarked Duyck, unlocking a wall cellaret and taking out a bottle and glass. "Always resist temptation. I always do. Till there isn't any resistance left."

"Good night, old chap," said Brenner, "and thanks for giving me a chance to win the rug. It was white of you."

"I gave you your one best chance just now when I turned my back on you to drink," hiccuped Duyck. "Why didn't you grab the rug and run for it? You could have made a very clean getaway."

"You had won the rug from me. Won it fairly. I'm no welcher."

"*Fairly?*" scoffed Duyck. "Here, my crank friend, take your silly

rug and clear out. I'm blessed if I can guess your game. But you're a man and a sportsman. I've tried you by every stunt I could think of. And you strike twelve every time. 'Won the rug *fairly*,' did I? Look here!"

He caught up the cards, ran his fingers through them, and began to throw poker hands on the table with bewildering rapidity.

And such hands! Full houses, fours, flushes, straights—at will. He wound up the performance by dealing a royal flush.

"What chance had you?" he laughed. "Candy from a baby! Mulcting the ultimate consumer! I can throw hands like those till doomsday, or till my wrist breaks.

"I guess you're too much of a man yourself to need me to explain that I'm never cur enough to do it except for fun. A knack an ocean liner shark taught me when I was a kid. After he'd bled me for a year's allowance. It's my only accomplishment. That and keeping the distilleries from closing down. Take your rug."

Brenner choked down a gust of anger at having been the butt of a youth for whom he had felt only an amused contempt. He picked up the rug and turned to the door.

"There's your fifteen dollars," said he, pointing to the money on the floor.

But Duyck was already filling his glass again.

"I will now indulge in a curious custom," quoth he, "which the Fiji Islanders have borrowed from the ancient Visigoths, who, in turn, are believed to have learned it from the Phenicians. I will accept my hospitable invitation to have just one more drink."

He suited the action to the word. When he spoke again the momentary clearness was gone from voice and brain.

"G'night, O seeker of adventures for the criminally insane," he babbled. "Be off, I prythee, while the offing is still at its best."

Filling his glass, he broke into song:

"Oh, I had a little hen, with little wooden legs,
And she supplied our table with the choicest wooden eggs.
She's the wisest little chicken we've got around the farm,
And an—anozzer li'l drink won' do us any harm!"

Galvin Brenner left his host testing the truth of his song's last line.

Down-stairs he went, the rug over his arm.

And in the foyer he came face to face with a severe-looking man in black. With this personage was a policeman.

"You see, constable," the man was saying apologetically, "Mr. Duyck—I'm his valet—is out of town to-night. And when I came home just now and found the street door standing wide open, I fancied perhaps some—"

He broke off. Brenner had seen the two new arrivals too late to duck out of sight. He stood, before their double gaze, on the stairway's lowest step, the rug conspicuously on his arm.

"I was right!" cried the valet. "Look, constable!"

The policeman had not only looked but leaped. Pistol drawn, he was upon Brenner. The valet, close behind, had caught up a heavy walking stick.

Brenner, not being a born fool, made no move to escape, but stood smiling debonairly at the excited pair.

"Put down that gun, officer," he suggested blandly. "It might go off. I don't think poor old Duyck would care to have me killed all over his foyer rug. And speaking of rugs—"

"'E's a thief, constable!" declaimed the valet. "Take 'im in custody!"

"What are you doin' here?" asked the policeman.

"Being held up, apparently," laughed Brenner, "I—"

"What were you doin' with that rug?"

"Van Cleek Duyck just gave it to me. I took a fancy to it and—"

"And to the plate as well, I'll warrant!" chimed in the valet. "Constable, Mr. Duyck never—"

"Come!" broke in Brenner with the air of a man who tires of a comic situation too long drawn out. "We'll step upstairs, all three, and Dr. Duyck will clear up the matter in a single word."

He turned and led the way upward; the two others trailing doubtfully and sullenly after him.

"My master is from home, constable!" cried the valet suddenly, as they neared the bedroom door. "I forgot, for the moment. This is a trick. An ambush, maybe. He—"

Brenner had stepped into the room. The policeman followed at a bound, as if fearing his prey was trying to escape. The valet followed

more cautiously.

There, stretched at full length across the foot of the bed, sprawled Van Cleek Duyck, having passed into peaceful slumber.

CHAPTER XI.

Desperate Remedies.

AT sight of Duyck the valet started right dramatically. Forgetful of the main issue, he explained:

"In all his clothes, too! 'Orrible! 'E'll want 'is ice water the instant he wakes up. 'E always does after such times."

The servant darted into the adjoining room whence presently issued the sound of chipping ice and splashing water.

Meantime, Brenner had seized Duyck by the shoulder and was shaking him with mighty vigor.

"Wake up and explain!" he shouted.

Van Cleek Duyck opened one eye and smiled serenely up at the policeman.

"My name's Norval-on-the-Grampian-Hills, off'cer," he cooed. "And you'll find the cash for my fine in my right hand trousers pocket. Keep th' change."

"Duyck!" clamored Brenner, renewing the shaking. "Wake up!"

Thus adjured, Van Cleek Duyck wearily raised himself on one elbow and gazed about him.

"Mr. Duyck," appealed the patrolman, pointing to Brenner, "do you know this man? Did you give him this rug? He claims to be a friend of yours."

Steadfastly and coldly, Van Cleek Duyck stared at Brenner. He looked him up and down with an impartial and judicial gravity.

At last he spoke:

"Never set eyes on th' fellow in my life," he announced, disinterestedly.

Then, pillowing his head on his arm he went to sleep again. He was not overcome by drink, but merely desired to slumber. And he

was a man who followed his desires.

"I guess that settles it," said the policeman, again drawing forth his revolver and with it a pair of handcuffs. "The 'gentleman burglar' stunt is about wore out, anyway!"

At sight of the highly business-like handcuffs and pistol, the valet set down the ice water pitcher he was bearing into the bedroom and prepared to enjoy the final scene of the "crook melodrama," in which he was privileged to play so smug a part.

Brenner was swayed by a rage that set every nerve in his body tingling. This drunken freak of Duyck's memory was likely to rob him of both rug and liberty. To have won so easily, and now to be arrested for a theft he had not committed, was the crowning stroke of ill luck.

Rage and the crying need to do something at once, if the desperate situation was to be saved, lashed Brenner into prompt action. His eye fell on the brimming ice water pitcher, and the spectacle brought inspiration.

Even as the policeman advanced, Brenner called out in sharp authority:

"Wait! One moment, you!"

And, before the officer could interfere or guess his intent, he had snatched up the pitcher.

At a single gesture he reversed it; sending a half gallon of ice-cold water cascading down over the slumberous Duyck's head and neck.

The valet cried out in horror. The patrolman, dimly scenting assault, leveled his revolver and ordered:

"Drop that and hold up your hands."

Brenner obeyed. He dropped the empty silver pitcher on Duyck's face.

"All right, officer," he said cheerily. "I'm just trying to bring Mr. Duyck back to his senses long enough to convince him that he knows me. If all that water, and the pitcher, too, can't do it, nothing can. See, he's coming around."

And, indeed, under the inundation of cold water and the sharp blow, Van Cleek Duyck had come back from dreamland on wings of haste. He was far more indifferent than drunk, and had merely returned to slumber as a means of avoiding noisy questions.

He had already struggled, gasping and sputtering, to a sitting

posture. The valet was making frantic dabs at his streaming head and face with a bath towel.

Duyck brushed aside the servant's loving ministrations and got to his feet. Dripping, choking, swearing, he glared about him like a wet hen.

"Well!" cried Brenner in the quick incisive tone that doctors employ in speaking to the delirious. "Are you sober, yet? Sober enough to get me out of this muddle? "

"What's that?" asked Duyck crossly. "Who poured all this water on me?"

"I did."

"I like your nerve. For two cents I'd punch your ugly head for it. Why in blazes did you try such a fresh kid joke as that?"

"To sober you up. I—"

"What right had you to sober me up? Did I ask you to? I didn't want to be sobered up, yet. I—"

"But I wanted you to be. If I hadn't brought you to your senses I'd be on my way to the police station by now."

"It's where you belong. It's where any man belongs who pours ice water on a man and then pounds him over the head! Hello, what's the cop doing here?"

"If you please, Mr. Duyck, sir," began the valet. "I came home and found—"

"The cop," interposed Brenner, "is here to arrest me for stealing. He caught me leaving the house with this rug you gave me. I told him how I got it. He wouldn't believe me. He asked you. You were tipsy and you denied any knowledge of me. I had to wake you up, unless I wanted to be jugged for theft."

"I see."

For a whole minute Duyck sat, face in hands on the bed-edge, the water still dripping mournfully from him.

Then he looked up, first at Brenner, then at the policeman. And his look and his voice bore no trace of drunkenness.

Yet Brenner held his breath. For it was quite within the range of possibility that the shock of awakening might have driven from the sleeper's mind any memory of the evening's events.

"Officer," said Duyck at last. "Thanks for looking out so well for

my interests. But it's all right. This is a friend of mine. I gave him the rug. Here is a little something to pay you for your trouble. Good night. Hardin," to the valet, "show the officer out. Then come back here and change me into dry clothes."

The appeased policeman and the still incensed valet departed.

Duyck turned on Brenner, speaking with swift incisiveness.

"I don't know you from Adam," said he. "And I don't understand any of this—how I chanced to give you a rug or how you happened to be here at all. But any idiot can see you're telling the truth. I'm afraid I was a bit misty.

"It's all right. Come back and explain when you feel like it. Have a drink? No? Well, good luck! I'm glad it was only a rug and not my strong box I gave you."

CHAPTER XII.

In the Lair of the Newlyweds.

IN the week that followed, Galvin Brenner called three times upon Ulrich Laing. Each time he bore with him one of the forty Ali Babas.

Once he brought a pair. And each time Laing favored the trophy with that same look of hopeful inquiry.

Yes, and always the glint of eager expectancy died in the rug king's little eyes as he caught a closer view.

Then he would nod approval. And with the air of a child awaiting a bedtime story he would lean back to hear the tale of his emissary's newest adventure.

Brenner fell to noticing that tense look of interrogation and the ensuing well-controlled twinge of disappointment. It set him to wondering.

Presumably the rugs, though of different patterns, were all of equal value. And it puzzled him that his employer should show chagrin whenever a glance at one of the rugs showed him the apparent absence of a mysterious something which he seemed to be expecting.

What this "something" might be, Brenner could not fathom.

Which irritated him, as time went on.

He had now brought Laing six rugs. Besides those acquired from Cauler, Father Curran, and Duyck were three more.

Two had been abstracted from a reception room in a garish uptown hotel by a man dressed in a porter's livery and carrying a hand vacuum-cleaner.

No one had objected; even when the porter had walked unconcernedly out of the big caravansary with his plunder.

For not only uniform, but livery as well, carries with it a mighty weight of law-abiding authority—in New York.

Next day the hotel's proprietor was perplexed to receive by mail a "John Doe" money order for thirty dollars. With the order was a typewritten slip of paper reading:

To 2 Ali Baba Rugs (benevolently assimilated) at $15 per. Total $30.
Account closed.

The third rug had well-nigh caused its captor's downfall.

Brenner had traced it to a mansion of gingerbread flats, high in the Bronx. There, his underground investigations had showed him, dwelt an uncommonly newly-wedded couple named Faune.

Indeed, they had been married but four days when Brenner honored them with his visit. The rug had been a wedding gift from a rich but cautious aunt.

Being poor both in money and leisure, the Faunes had wasted neither of these scant commodities in a honeymoon trip. They had gone at once from the church to their new home.

And next morning the groom had returned to his office, after only a single day's absence.

His wife had a way of walking to the subway station, two long blocks distant, every afternoon to meet him on his return from down-town. He always managed to catch the same train and reached the Bronx at exactly 5.46.

This then (as the couple kept no maid) was the psychological hour for Brenner's furtive call.

Thither, accordingly, on the afternoon of the fifth day, he repaired.

He reached the house at just eighteen minutes before five, suitcase in hand, climbed five flights of stairs (the only reason the Faunes lived

on the fifth floor was because there was no sixth) and halted before the varnished door of their flat.

He figured that he had at least a full five minutes to search for the rug, secure it, and depart.

Running a thin knife-blade between the metal door-jamb and its wooden side-strip, he pressed back the lock with ridiculous ease—as flat thieves have done by thousands ever since the first "gingerbread" apartment house was built—and turned the knob.

The architecture of such places is of a painful sameness. Also, poor people with presumably only one handsome rug are prone to keep that same rug in the living-room.

So, unerringly, Galvin Brenner turned to the left and made his way down the short, twisted hall to the living-room. And there, on the floor, in front of the cheap, lightwood upright piano, was the rug.

Moreover, at various points, littering the ill-varnished floor, were other rugs. A full dozen, of all sizes and all degrees of sleazy ugliness, overlapping one another from sheer numbers.

Brenner had neither time nor desire to enter upon a closer inspection of this phenomenal rug crop in so small a space. He stepped into the room, his foot falls wholly deadened by the multitude of floor coverings, and made his way toward the rug he wanted.

As he did so, the sound of voices broke in on his plans. Two women were coming down the hall from the rear of the apartment.

Brenner slipped behind the scrim curtains that parted the living-room from the adjacent bedroom.

He shoved his suitcase under a chair, for he knew he would probably have to depart in a hurry when he should find a chance to go at all. And a bulky suitcase is not an aid to rapid flight.

He swept the neat little bedroom with a single glance. There was no other means of egress except that leading into the living-room.

The folding bed was up. That would offer no shelter. Nor was there a spot in the entire tiny room where a child could have hidden.

The women had well-nigh reached the living-room. Brenner's faint hope that they might go out of the flat door was quickly dispelled. For, as he crouched behind the flimsy curtains, he heard them enter the room he had just quitted.

From the scraps of talk he subconsciously heard, he gathered that

Mrs. Faune was showing a girl friend over the apartment, and he heartily cursed her negligence in choosing this day, of all others, for breaking her new custom of going to meet her husband.

"I left my wrist-bag in your bedroom, I think," observed the guest, as they left the hall. "I'll go in and get it. Then it'll surely be time to meet Carl. He'd never forgive me if I made you late."

"Oh, I've lots of time," returned the bride. "See, my watch says just half-past four."

"Oh, women's watches!" groaned Brenner to himself. "I used to think it was a joke that they never keep time. Now I see it's a tragedy!"

"Let me get the bag for you," went on the bride, taking a step toward the bedroom, evidently as a measure to speed the parting guest.

But the latter had caught sight of the brave if motley array of carpeting.

"Bess!" exclaimed she, trying to stifle a laugh. "Every time I come here I feel as if I were in a rug shop. And now that the afternoon sun shows them up so plainly—"

"*Plainly?*" echoed her hostess. "Say, rather, *hideously!* Don't laugh. I feel more like crying. Our own pretty rugs are in the other room. These are the 'gift rugs.'

"I read a funny story once about a bride who got twenty-seven berry spoons and all of them marked, so she couldn't exchange them. But thirteen rugs as wedding presents are even worse. Thirteen rugs! Carl says he'll strangle the next person that dares to send us one.

"I could stand the other twelve; but the rug over in front of the piano I take as a personal insult. Aunt Maida gave it to us. She is so rich she can afford to be stingy. But I'm her only niece, and I certainly thought she'd give us at least a check for a hundred dollars when we were married. She knows how hard up we were and what a wonderful difference a hundred dollars would make to us at this time."

"And she actually sent you nothing but that homely rug?"

"Not a blessed thing. Carl says it's so ugly that maybe it's a magic carpet. I think some time I'll stand in front of it and wish for it to change itself into a hundred-dollar bill. I—Oh!" she broke short in dismay, "my watch is *stopped!* That's why it's so early. I must have forgotten to—"

"Quick! He'll be so disappointed if you're not there. I'll get my bag.

Oh, I remember now. I left it in the dining-room. I put it on the sideboard there, when we were folding up the tablecloth the Cantons gave you. I'll—"

Together they raced down the hall. Brenner, in one bound, was in the living-room.

He snatched up the rug, laid a hundred-dollar bill in its place, and bolted for the door.

"There's *one* woman who'll believe in magic all the rest of her days!" he chuckled under his breath, as he noiselessly let himself out of the apartment and shut the door behind him. "And I guess it's a hundred dollars mighty well spent."

He flung the rug over his shoulder and started for the stairs. A man was toiling up the last flight.

"That you, Bess?" called the climber hearing Brenner's light footfall. "You were late."

He looked up, but not before Brenner had had time to wheel about and approach the flat's door again.

The householder thus beheld a man engaged in deciphering the name-card on the door.

Then he caught sight of the rug that hung over the stranger's shoulder, and he bristled like a fighting dog.

"Who are you looking for?" he challenged.

Brenner turned, his face meek and stupid.

"I'm looking for C. L. Fame's apartment," he mumbled. "I got a rug to deliver here."

"You have, hey?" thundered the bridegroom. "Well, unless you want to be thrown down-stairs and then walked on, you'll turn around and carry that rug so far away it'll discover a new street. Chase, now!"

"But," pleaded Brenner, "they gimme orders to deliver—"

"This is my flat," stormed Faune, "and no more of those horrible rugs go into it except over my dead body. Why," with a second look at the Ali Baba, "I've got one already of something the same pattern as that. And it's so ugly I have to lock it up in the kitchen at night. I'm not going to harbor another one like it. Take the thing away! And—"

The flat door opened and the bride and her friend emerged.

At sight of Faune, both waxed incoherently voluble; each explaining in a different key the reason for the delay in starting for the

subway station.

And under cover of the triangular volley of babble, Galvin Brenner quietly walked down-stairs, bearing the rejected rug triumphantly in front of him.

"I'd give a lot," he mused, "to see these Newlyweds' faces when they find the hundred dollars—and a new suitcase!"

CHAPTER XIII.

In "Millionaires' Row."

AS Brenner finished the recital of his escape from the newlyweds, Laing observed patronizingly:

"You were quite right in saying that half the cleverness employed in theft would make a man a success in any honest line. But half the bad luck you've had in this quest would have swamped any square man's business interests."

"I suppose so."

"Except when you got those two rugs from the Hotel St. Crœsus," added Laing, "you've had the narrowest sort of escape every time. And as there are six more rugs to get, one of two things will happen: either your run of bad luck will break, or else you'll find yourself behind bars.

"And," he ended with a twinge of anxiety, "if you *do* get locked up, remember our bargain: you're not to bring my name into it."

"That's understood. I'm no squealer."

"Even if you were," said Laing uneasily, "it would do you no good. It would be your bare word against mine. The word of a self-confessed crook against an established business man's. No one would believe you."

"My friend," drawled Brenner, "I suppose the only thing that kept you from many a thrashing is the fact that you've no idea how offensive you are. Ignorance is easily forgiven. But let that go. You're right in one thing. I *have* had a rotten run of luck, so far as discovery is concerned. The worst I've ever had.

"I suppose it's because I've turned square! When I was a real thief my good luck was a byword: I could get away with chances no other chap would dare to take. It's queer how fortune changes when a man is trying to keep straight."

"Perhaps," suggested Laing with elephantine playfulness under which seemed to lurk a trace of sincerity, "if you'd managed at each place to steal some little trifle for yourself, as well as the rug, you might be luckier. It might break the hoodoo."

"As I just told you," smiled Brenner, rising to go, "your ignorance of your own offensiveness saves you from a lot of hospital treatment."

"Where next?" questioned Laing, in no wise offended.

"I'll tell you after I come back. It is always my one unbreakable rule to tell my plans—*afterward*—in case they succeed. Because, then, if they don't, no one can guy me for failing."

Up the servants' stairway of an architectural crime, that stood in a line of similar mansions known to the newspapers as "Millionaires' Row," climbed Galvin Brenner.

On his vest lapel under cover of his coat was an electric light inspector's badge. In his pocket was a credential card from a light company.

These matters are not wholly difficult to arrange when one knows how. And Brenner, like many another notable of the underworld, "knew how."

The rightful owner of these credentials and of the empty black kit-bag Brenner carried, was twenty dollars richer for their temporary loan. He had lent them before on the same terms, and always on the following morning they had been faithfully restored to him.

The kit-bag was no part of a regular inspector's equipment. But no householder would note that discrepancy.

The hour was early—barely eight o'clock. General Clyde Irwin, owner of the house—and of a seven-figure fortune and the finest private art collection in the Western world—was giving a heavily formal dinner to many fellow-magnates and art patrons.

Thus there was but little life just now in the servants' living quarters or in any part of the big house save in the dining-room, kitchen and butler's pantry. On the dinner's success was bent the thoughts and

energies of the whole household, both the above and below-stairs' contingents.

Brenner moved peacefully up the servants' staircase to a suite of rooms on the third floor. There he wandered forth into a sort of foyer and set to work tinkering at an electric light bracket.

The houseman, detailed thereto by the butler, was at his heels and stood watching him at work with a stolid suspicion.

This mildly annoyed Brenner. He knew he should have to get rid of the fellow. And he knew this would be no easy task. For he recognized the type of human bulldog, not over-clever, but vigilant and innately suspicious of every middle-class stranger who chanced to enter his employer's house.

The obvious plan of knocking the houseman in the head and thus, for a time, causing his guardian interest to flag, incurred too much danger, for there might still be people in that part of the house.

Indeed, even as he dismissed such an idea, Brenner heard the swish of a woman's skirt crossing a near-by room.

The temporary "inspector" had some general idea as to electricity. With great show of competence he proceeded to dismantle the bracket-light and to examine its wiring.

Meantime he furtively used his eyes. Not in search of the rug he sought. He had discovered that the moment he entered the foyer.

He was in a wing of the house apparently devoted to the quarterings of such superior employees as housekeeper, household secretary, governess, and trained nurse. The servants' quarters, he had learned, were on the floor above.

The foyer in which Brenner was working was fitted up as a lounging-room. Its furnishings were tasteful, even in a way luxurious. The Irwins evidently believed in making their "upper staff" comfortable.

From the foyer opened several adjacent rooms, presumably bedrooms. It was in one of these that Brenner had heard the woman moving about.

The rug he sought lay before a wide table at one end of the foyer. The table itself was littered with several neatly tied packages and with a quantity of loose wrapping-paper and string.

"Queer time of year for putting up Christmas presents," he observed, with labored jocularity, to the houseman. "It's a real privilege

to see how rich people do their Christmas shopping early."

"H-m!" grunted the houseman.

"It's some months before Christmas," went on Brenner, his tone shifting adroitly from badinage to stupid curiosity. "I s'pose at this rate, by the time Christmas comes, that table will be piled up pretty near to the ceiling. Or maybe millionaires celebrate Christmas *earlier* than other folks."

As he had hoped, the glum houseman fell into the trap baited with the love of displaying superior knowledge.

"Those ain't Christmas presents, you simp!" he scoffed. "They're birthday presents."

"No?" exclaimed Brenner, his mouth agape with wonder. "Do rich folks celebrate all their birthdays at the same time? Gee, but I'm learning a lot, trailing along with a live wire like you, sir!"

"Mr. Irwin," corrected the houseman, obviously pleased with the other's admiration—"Mr. Irwin's birthday is to-morrow. Every year, on his birthday, he sends a present to each of his twenty-year employees down on Broad Street. The secretary's been putting them up this afternoon. They go by parcel post to-night. Now, suppose you go ahead with your work? I can't have my dinner till you go."

Brenner bent once more to his inspection of the wires. The houseman, frittering around impatiently, chanced to pick up the kit-bag Brenner had left on the table.

"Pretty light," he commented.

"It's empty," replied Brenner. "I brought it on from the last house I went to. I used up the last wire coil there."

"Brought it empty, hey? Well, I'll just dip into it when you go out to make sure you carry it away empty, too. No offense. I'm responsible. The butler put it up to me."

"Sure!" agreed Brenner. "And when I go you can frisk my clothes, too, in case you think I've palmed a grand piano or a mahogany sideboard and slipped it under my vest."

He spoke as lightly as though every atom of his superalert brain were not at that instant strained to the utmost in readjusting his plans to meet this new difficulty.

A summons from below stairs forced the reluctant houseman out of the room. On departing he ostentatiously locked behind him every

door leading into the foyer and pocketed the keys. "No offense," he repeated as he did so.

"None at all!" laughed Brenner. "It's your job."

"I'll be back in a minute," mumbled the half-ashamed man. "They only want me to—"

He was gone, leaving Brenner snugly locked in.

Before he was half-way down the first flight Brenner was at the package-laden table. He snatched up the rug and a big sheet of wrapping-paper.

Deftly and with the furtive speed of the light-fingered, he wrapped the rug in a neat parcel. With his fountain pen he scribbled on it his own name and address in a fair imitation of the housekeeper's flowing, public-school chirography on the other bundles.

Returning footsteps warned him his time was short. He had barely time to thrust the package (address side down) among the others on the table and step back to the wires, when the houseman reappeared.

"Say," Brenner greeted him sourly, "I've been thinking it over, and I'll not stick on a job where I'm taken for a thief—see? The company can send somebody else. Search the bag and be damned to you! And let me out o' here."

CHAPTER XIV.

Treasure Trove.

WHEN Galvin Brenner went downstairs to breakfast at his boarding-house next morning he found in the lower hall a bulky parcel-post package addressed to him.

It was the rug from the Irwin mansion.

Carrying it to his room, he undid it, glanced it over to make certain of its identity, put it in a satchel, and proceeded to address an envelope to "Gen. Irwin, Irwin Building, 9999 Broad Street, New York City."

Into the envelope he placed a blank sheet of paper and three five-dollar bills. He mailed it at the corner before going back to breakfast.

Forty Ali Babas and a Thief

An hour later he walked into Ulrich Laing's office, drew out the rug from the satchel, and laid it on the desk.

Whereupon the portly and dignified Mr. Ulrich did a right unseemly thing.

After one look at the rug spread before him he emitted a whoop that resounded through the whole building.

He followed this with a war-dance all around the room, capering from end to end of the office with the dreamy, sensuous grace of an ice-wagon that has lost a left front wheel.

He wound up the performance by hurling both arms around the dumfounded Brenner's neck and bestowing upon that disgusted young man a genuine bear hug.

"Why in blazes do you drink so early in the morning?" snorted Brenner, forcibly disengaging himself, "Or is it acute mania?"

"It's neither, my dear boy!" exulted Laing, seizing the rug and gloating over it—after the fashion made popular by Gaspard the miser. "It's neither. I'm the happiest man in all this little old burg. You see this rug? Well, it spells 'T-r-e-a-s-u-r-e' to me. We've won, lad! We've won!

"Oh, I knew I was making no mistake in giving you a crack at the job! No, nor in following my hunch in hiring you in the first place. Something told me to. I have few hunches. But they never fail me!"

"Mr. Laing," cautioned Brenner, half contemptuously, "if the sight of the seventh missing rug affects you this way I'm afraid by the time I bring in the twelfth you'll—"

"The twelfth!" scoffed Laing. "Son, your quest is over. Let the rest of 'em slide. I've got what I wanted. I—"

"You mean to say you aren't going to bother about recovering five rugs, each of them worth more than a thousand dollars?" cried the amazed Brenner. "You're content to lose more than five thousand dollars, and—"

"Five thousand cork legs!" chuckled Laing. "Brenner, my lad, none of those rugs were worth more than about twenty-five dollars at the outside. A hundred dollars would cover the lot. And I'll square that by tacking it on to my bill. Yes, and I'll give you a thousand-dollar bonus for myself. And you'll start here to-day on a salary of forty dollars a week.

"You're a valuable man. I'll find other delicate bits of work for you

to do as time goes on."

"One moment, please!" interposed Brenner, a steely glint beginning to show in his eyes. "There are one or two things I don't clearly understand. You told me once that those rugs were worth more than a thousand dollars apiece. And now you say—"

"So they were, Brenner. So they were. But they aren't any more."

"The rug market surely couldn't fluctuate enough in that short time to lower values by ninety-seven and a half per cent."

"Clever chap! But you're mistaken. It could. It has. That bundle of forty rugs, as it reached me, was worth not forty thousand dollars, but more than one hundred and forty thousand. Minus one certain rug it was worth less than one thousand. And this is the one certain rug. See the idea? And, now that I have this, the others can be used as floor-cloths, for all I care."

"If you had told me," began Brenner coldly, "that there was only one rug you wanted back—"

"You'd have gathered the idea that it was a treasure and bolted with it the second you could lay hands on it. There, there, man! Keep your collar on! I didn't mean to offend you. I only meant I couldn't take chances when a thing was so precious. So I worked it out a safer way. Don't be hurt. I apologize for doubting you. It won't happen again."

Brenner stood looking at the rug king in angry indecision. Laing, uncomfortable at the possible menace in his employee's scowl, hastened to change the topic.

"You've told me some mighty entertaining stories of your adventures lately," said he. "Now it's my turn. And, after all you've done for me, it's only fair you should know the whole affair. I think it will interest you."

CHAPTER XV.

The Story of the Amina.

BRENNER hesitated. Then, curiosity getting the better of pique, he sat down.

After his many conjectures and perplexities on the subject it would

be interesting to have the mystery cleared and to learn the cause of his stolid employer's wild excitement on losing and on recovering the rug.

Laing settled back in his desk-chair, the treasured bit of oriental carpeting across his knees.

"This," he said, stroking it lovingly, "is the Amina rug."

He made the announcement as though he were exhibiting the Koh-i-noor at the very least. To Brenner the words meant nothing.

Laing, noting his hearer's blank and unimpressed look, frowned.

"I forgot," he snapped. "I forgot I was talking to an ignoramus in rugs. Any one in the trade—and any collector—would have been thunderstruck at what I've just told you. But then any such person would have recognized the Amina at a glance from its pictures just as easily as the man in the street would recognize Theodore Roosevelt."

"Quite so," retorted Brenner. "We'll admit my blank ignorance. Go ahead."

"Though you may not remember hearing of the Amina rug," resumed Laing with the air of an indulgent teacher coaching a mental defective, "you'll have no trouble tracing the origin of its name by the fact that it's called 'Amina.'"

"Oh, of course!" answered Brenner, irritated. "Amina of course— Amina. How silly of me not to have thought! Good old Amina!

"And while we're on the subject suppose you tell me whether an Amina is a dog or a bird or a patent medicine. Or is he a celebrity over in the East? Maybe over there they name their rugs as we name our five-cent cigars?"

Ulrich Laing held up both fat hands as though at gross sacrilege.

"Amina," he said in stern reproof, "was the mother of the prophet. I thought every one—"

"What profit?"

"The Prophet Mohammed."

"Oh! And they named this brand of rugs after her?"

"*Brand* of rugs?" gasped Laing. "Mr. Brenner, there is no duplicate anywhere of the Amina rug. It rested under the head of the prophet's mother during her last illness—"

"I hope she didn't have anything contagious," muttered Brenner, moving back a little.

"And ever since," continued, Laing, "it has been the highest object

of veneration in the mosque of Ali at Teheran in Persia. Apart from its history, its workmanship is a miracle of art. It is the finest example of 'single weave' in all the Hegira epoch. The secret of that warp was lost centuries ago. It—"

"Yes?" said Brenner, to whom much of this glowing description was mere jargon. "But why didn't you tell me all this at the start? You needn't have been afraid of my stealing it, as you so tactfully hinted, just now.

"For, if the rug's appearance is so familiar to every dealer and collector, the theft could have been traced at once. A stolen rug isn't like a stolen diamond. It can't be cut up or reset.

"If you'd told me and shown a picture of this rug I could have made the rounds, simply looking at each, without trying to take it till I came to the right one. It would have averted a lot of danger and saved a lot of time."

"I know," admitted Laing, "I know. It was a mistake. I see it now. By the way, where did you get it?"

"Among the names on the delivery list was Mrs. Howson, on Fifth Avenue," answered Brenner. "I looked her up and found she was housekeeper in a big Wall Street man's family. People of that class don't send their housekeepers to choose the furnishings for their homes. Only for the 'below-stairs' region.

"The rug was too costly for the servants' rooms, so I knew it must be meant for the housekeeper's own quarters or the quarter allotted to the upper employees of the family. That's where I looked, and that's where I found it."

"Clever boy! And the man who footed the bill never guessed what a treasure his housekeeper had bought for him!"

"Naturally not. I don't suppose he would potter around the servants' quarters, taking inventories of the furniture. A man like General Irwin doesn't waste much time on—"

A veritable howl of amazement and mirth from Laing interrupted him.

The rug king rocked back and forth, purple of face, doubled up with Homeric laughter, slapping his fat knees and stamping. He looked helplessly up at Brenner with convulsed face and streaming eyes.

"Oh!" he squeaked breathlessly. "You'll be the death of me yet!"

And off he went into another paroxysm.

"I see," observed Brenner, battling with a yearning to take Laing over his knee and spank him, "I see I have missed my vocation. In vaudeville I should have made a fortune. I must be what is known as an unconscious humorist."

"Irwin!" wheezed the apoplectic Laing, "Irwin! Irwin, of all men! Oh!"

A joke is one of the few good things in life that even the most selfish man is always eager to share with the whole world. And presently Laing choked back his spasms of merriment, wiped his trickling eyes and continued pantingly:

"Listen, my friend, you must hear the rest of the Amina rug's history."

"Thanks. It doesn't interest me."

"But it *will*. Wait till you hear the point. Just listen:

"For centuries the Amina has been the cynosure of every rug-lover's eye. Thousands of collectors have made the long journey to Teheran for no other reason than to feast their eyes on it. To—"

"On that dull-looking scrap of carpet? Well, every man to his own taste. Go on."

"The Persian government has been offered unbelievable sums for it. Millionaires, grand dukes, museums—all have made enormous bids for it. But religious relics are the only things that a Moslem holds more sacred than money. The Amina is one of the most precious relics in the East, and Persia regarded all offers for its sale as dire insults."

"I don't wonder."

"Since it was found no money could buy the treasure," went on Laing, "the most daring efforts have been made from time to time to get it by other means."

"To steal it?"

"If one puts it in that brutal way. But it can scarcely be called 'stealing' to remove a wonderful object of art from a set of bigoted Mohammedans and giving its hidden beauty to the world."

"I see," dryly commented Brenner. "Most dips and yeggs feel that way about your rich men's cash. Well, if the rug wasn't for sale, and—"

"It was guarded like crown jewels," said Laing. "Every effort to get it was blocked. More than one plucky adventurer has lost his life

trying to—"

"But why? What would be the sense of stealing a thing that was so well known? The thief or the man who bought it from him wouldn't dare to boast that he had it. He'd have to keep it hidden or show it only to a few friends he could trust."

"Brenner," smiled Laing, "I'm afraid you don't quite understand the 'collector's spirit'—the spirit that makes a man pay a fortune for an object of art, just for the bliss of knowing that it belongs to *him*. But that spirit exists in hundreds of collectors. How else account for the vanishing of the 'Gainsborough,' the 'Mona Lisa,' the—"

"I know," rejoined Brenner, "I had the collector's spirit myself once. So have lots of Americans who aren't millionaires. They have a club for such men, called Sing Sing. And another at Auburn. And another—"

"A dozen schemes have been set afoot," continued Laing, unheeding, "to get hold of the Amina. Several rich men have had standing offers out for the rug. This year one of those schemers succeeded. The rug was won. Right under the noses of its guardians."

"Stolen? "

"Captured. It was brought to my agent in Teheran. He knew I had been on the lookout for it for the past ten years. Not for myself, of course. But because a New York patron of arts made me a standing offer of one hundred and fifty thousand dollars for the Amina if I could get it for him."

"But—"

"I cabled cipher instructions to my agent over there the minute I got the word from him. And I notified the New Yorker who stood ready to buy it. The rug was wrapped up in my regular monthly consignment from Teheran and sent to me openly.

"The open way was the only safe way. The customs people at both ends—there and Persia—are used to handling my rugs. In all my business career I've never tried to smuggle anything. And they know it.

"So they don't examine my stuff overclosely. I pay a regular yearly sum in Persia not to have my rugs mauled over or roughly handled.

"No one would suspect the missing Amina was in a bundle that any one could open or loot. It was a good idea.

"I went in person to the dock to get the rugs. But, as I told you, the boat arrived an hour ahead of schedule. Caton knew nothing of my big deal. So he got the consignment through the custom-house and shipped it up here, where you sold a dozen of the rugs. The Amina was among them.

"Now you can see why I was a bit excited. The buyer waiting, wild to get his treasure and pay me my one hundred and fifty thousand dollars and expenses. The rug gone. It was enough to rattle any man.

"Here comes the joke—the cream of all the jokes ever heard. The New York man commissioned me to get the Amina for him and who was wild over the delay was—*General Irwin!* And for a week or two the priceless rug was kicking about his own house, till you took it from there last night. Catch the point? He had it all the time—for fifteen dollars! The wonderful Amina!"

Again Laing exploded into laughter. Looking across to meet Brenner's grin of appreciation, the rug king suddenly stopped laughing.

For Galvin Brenner's face was gray and tense. His lips were set in a white line. From his eyes blazed the very devil of murder.

Laing scrambled to his feet, aghast. And for an instant the sudden fear of death seemed to leap into his plump face.

"Brenner!" he gasped. "What is it, man? What is it?"

CHAPTER XVI.

Thief and Thief.

FOR a moment Brenner made no reply. He stood, clenching and unclenching his hands, the hot glow of his eyes fairly searing the discomfited man before him.

Then the white lips parted and speech came—words thick with anger, at first almost incoherent.

"You crook!" snarled Galvin Brenner. "You *crook!* You've stolen—not the rug, but my honor—my honesty—my reform!"

"Wha'—what are you talking about?" bleated Laing, his hand on the bell. "Are you crazy?"

"Take your hand off that bell!" ordered Brenner, his voice little above a whisper. "You'll hear what I have to say. Take your hand off that bell, I tell you, or whoever answers it will find a dead man at your desk."

Laing withdrew his hand and essayed a laugh. It was not a success.

"You'll hear what I have to say," repeated Brenner. "I came to you for a chance to live square. To clean up the past. To be a decent man. I held back nothing of my past life from you. I asked you to give me a chance. I offered to work for next to nothing; to do anything that would give me the right to look decent men in the face."

"If this is a sermon—"

"It isn't. Be quiet. I made a blunder here. I sold a batch of rugs at the wrong time. I offered you every cent I had in the world to atone for that blunder. According to your own estimate, three hundred dollars would have more than paid the rugs' actual value.

"You lied to me. To make me recover the Amina rug for you you played on the fact that I was trying to be square, and you set me to work getting back the rug for you."

"Business, my boy! Business!" chuckled Laing, with a weak attempt at jauntiness.

"Business!" repeated Brenner. "Not a professional crook in all New York would have stooped to such 'business.' It had to be thought out by a reputable member of society—a rich, respected merchant! You tried to make me steal back those rugs. When you found I wouldn't, you eased my conscience by letting me pay for them—with my own cash."

"I offered—"

"And all the time," burst forth Brenner, his voice rumbling in his throat like the growl of an angry dog, "all the time you were making a thief of me! A *thief!* Laughing to yourself to think how you were using my strength for honesty to help you win back a treasure that you'd worse than stolen!"

"My dear boy! We—"

"I was trying to live square, and what have you tricked me into doing? You have made me a party to a bigger, more outrageous theft than all I ever committed in my whole career as a crook. You made me help steal a treasure worth one hundred and fifty thousand dollars! To

help you defraud a church—"

"A mosque," feebly corrected Laing. "It isn't like a—"

"It is the same thing. You made me help in the theft of something that millions of people regard as holy.

"It was stolen from a Mohammedan place of worship. That is the kind of theft that mighty few folk of the underworld would soil their hands with. You've used me in getting back that rug, so that you might sell it to a fellow thief—a receiver of stolen goods. And you think it a fine joke!"

"I—I was—"

"A fine joke to thrust back into the slime a man who was trying to crawl out onto firm ground and look his fellow man in the face once more. To make him share in a crime worse than any he had ever committed at his very worst.

"And because my wit has won you back your church-stolen plunder, you offer me forty dollars a week and one thousand dollars bonus! The price of smashed honor has boomed vastly since the primitive days of the thirty pieces."

"You are discharged!" blustered Laing. "No man is going to compare me to Judas Iscariot and get away with it. I—"

"With Judas?" mocked Brenner. "I didn't honor you by comparing you to him. Judas, as far as I know, dragged no one else into his crime. He soiled no hands but his own.

"You don't know," he went on, a little catch in his throat, "what my hopes of a straight life meant to me. And now—the whole dreary climb must begin all over again."

"I'm sorry you take this so hard," observed Laing, recovering his courage as the cold fury died out of Brenner's face and voice. "But after what you've said to me to-day of course I can't keep you in my employ; I am very busy. Good day."

He turned to his desk and reached once more toward his bell.

The next instant he was whirling across the room, through no volition of his own, and brought up against the farther wall with a thump that completely knocked the breath out of his body.

Before he could cry out a handkerchief was thrust deftly into his open mouth and his hands were pinioned behind his back.

Brenner, gripping both the struggling, imprisoned wrists in

his own left hand, ripped from the wall a shimmering antique rug. Putting one end of this under his heel he rent the rug into several long strips.

With these costly bonds he proceeded to tie the wriggling Ulrich Laing hand and foot, and to fasten a shorter strip around his head to keep the handkerchief gag in place.

"It's dangerous to have dealings with a former crook," observed Brenner grimly as he gazed down at the prisoner who writhed helplessly on the rug-strewn floor.

"But it is ten times more dangerous to try to double-cross him. You'll stay where you are till some one comes in to untie you. It won't be especially comfortable, but it is a lot more comfortable than jail— where you belong."

Brenner adjusted his tie which had been twisted during the brief scuffle. Then once more he addressed the gurgling Laing.

"You won't tell about this," announced Brenner, "because you can't without telling your own share in it. And that would mean prison for you and probably for Irwin as well. I'm quite safe from pursuit, so far as you are concerned. Good-by."

Brenner picked up the Amina rug from the desk, folded it neatly, put it back in the satchel and marched unconcernedly out of the office with it.

CHAPTER XVII.

The Amateur and the Diplomat.

TUFIK ALI AKBAR KHAN, *chargé d'affaires* in the United States for the serene and ancient sun-kingdom of Persia, was dressing in his Washington home for a White-House dinner.

His valet had arranged the last touches of his master's evening toilet and had left the room. The *charge d'affaires* glanced at himself in the pier glass, lighted a cigarette, and prepared to descend to his waiting car.

But before he could reach the door leading from his dressing-room

the door was opened and a man quietly stepped in.

The newcomer was in morning costume and carried a hand-bag. He had not troubled to knock on entering the room.

But now, as he closed the door behind him, he bowed and stood for an instant facing the amazed diplomat.

"Who are you?" demanded Tufik, somewhat sharply, "and who admitted you?"

"I was not admitted," answered the other. "In fact, I was told you could not receive me this evening and that you are leaving Washington for several days, the first thing in the morning. So I came in without permission."

"My servants—"

"Your servants are not to blame. They don't know I got in."

"Please go at once," requested Tufik, who scented a crank, a concession seeker, or a better-class mendicant. "My business hours are—"

"Are too far away to be of any use to me. Moreover, my errand is private. It concerns your country—"

"My business hours," repeated the *charge d'affaires*, "are—"

"It also concerns the Amina rug."

Tufik halted abruptly on his journey to the door. His dark face was suddenly alert.

But diplomat fashion he masked any show of interest and merely strolled back toward his visitor.

"Who are you?" he asked, "and what do you wish to know about the Amina rug? The encyclopedia will tell—"

"That it was stolen recently from the great mosque at Teheran? I think not. Not even the newspapers seem to know it. Your government has evidently kept the matter quiet."

"Who are *you?*"

"My name is Brenner. And I've brought back the Amina rug. Will you take it and give me a receipt?"

Tufik looked blankly at the strange guest—at the man who spoke thus familiarly of a theft which had stirred the very throne of Persia to the foundation; and which had been thus far kept as official secret, even from the Moslem world, lest wholesale riot and perchance even a holy war should result.

The loss of the sacred Amina rug from the great mosque had been

cabled in cipher to all of Persia's foreign representations; and fortunes had been spent in hiring detectives in every port of Europe and America to trace it.

Yet, up to now, the secret had remained close guarded from the public.

Even in Teheran the faithful were told that the Amina had been placed in the royal treasury and hidden for a time from the public gaze of devotees in order to avert a sacreligious plot of Russian emissaries to steal or deface it.

As a result, popular indignation against Russia boiled to white heat—which the Persian government desired it should—and the day of reckoning was for a spell delayed.

Yet, in private, the wheels of influence, of money, of private information, all over the world were turned by diplomatic zeal to discover the whereabouts of the stolen rug. Police agents of every land, dazzled by the enormous rewards offered, were scouring the underworld, putting known crooks through the third degree, following up a thousand clues.

And, after all this covert turmoil, a complete stranger dropped from nowhere into the dressing-room of Persia's *chargé d'affaires* at Washington and coolly offered to return the rug.

Much as he might have brought back a strayed dog!

Small wonder that even a veteran diplomat and Oriental like Tufik Khan was startled out of his perfect calm.

Meantime, Galvin Brenner had unfastened the clasps of the satchel and with profaning touch was hauling out of it, hand over hand, the holy rug.

It needed but a glance to tell Tufik that the rug was the lost and sacred Amina.

At the careless handling it was receiving from this infidel the Persian drew his breath quickly between set teeth. And his fingers itched.

But his were the breeding and the self-control that only the East can produce. And he stood inert while the sacrilege went on. He even forced a polite smile to his full lips.

Brenner, pleasantly unaware of the anguish he was evoking, pulled the rug from the bag, straightened it out and laid it on the polished floor.

"There you are!" he observed. "Good as new."

The Persian eyed him keenly, waiting the next move.

Here was a type that even a diplomat could not understand. If the fellow were the Amina's robber, why had he not sent emissaries to make terms and to demand a guarantee of immunity?

If he were not the thief but merely an intermediary, why did he bring the rug in person and lay it carelessly there at the feet of Persia's Washington representative?

The whole thing—from a commonsense as well as a diplomatic standpoint—was unintelligible. And, diplomatlike, Tufik waited for his adversary to make the next move.

"This is the rug, all right, isn't it?" queried Brenner, puzzled by his host's silence.

"It *is* the holy Amina," gravely assented Tufik with an inclination of the head.

"And you represent Persia in the United States just now, don't you?" continued Brenner. "I got here from New York half an hour ago. I called up a Washington man I know and he told me there's no Persian minister here at present and that you are the man in authority, so I came direct to you. You *are* at the head of the Persian Embassy in the United States, aren't you?"

"I am."

"Good. Then that's settled," answered Brenner, closing and clasping the satchel again. "I've brought the rug to the right place. I thought, first, of turning it over to the Persian consul-general in New York. His office is somewhere on Fifth Avenue, I believe. But I make it a rule always to deal direct. It's best to go straight to headquarters. So I came here. Now, if you'll give me a receipt—"

"A receipt?" asked the Persian.

"Yes. In case I'm suspected of having kept the Amina myself I want something to clear me."

"But," babbled Tufik, utterly out of his depth, "the reward—"

"What reward?"

Again Tufik felt he had run, head on, into a stone wall.

It was inconceivable that a man would have stolen or received the stolen Amina without also having learned or guessed that a princely reward awaited its restoration. And yet, any cub attache could have seen this man was sincere in his perplexity at the mention of payment.

Tufik tried another trick. He met simplicity with still greater

simplicity.

"When it was learned that the holy rug was gone from the mosque," he explained, "His Serene Majesty the Shah—on whom be peace!—offered a large sum of money as a reward for its return. You have returned it, and—"

"Oh!" laughed Brenner, "I see, I get the idea. Well, I'm not in the reward-hunting profession. I don't want any reward. Just a line from you, saying I brought the rug to you, as Persia's local representative, safely and in good shape."

Tufik Khan rang a bell. To the valet who appeared in answer to it—and who gazed in bewilderment at the presence of a stranger and a foreigner in his master's dressing-room—the *charge d'affaires* gave an order in Persian. The valet bowed and withdrew.

A moment later a young Persian in European evening dress appeared on the threshold. At sight of the Amina rug on the floor in front of him he gave a cry of wonder and made as though to prostrate himself before it.

Then, catching his chief's eye, he straightened himself and stood meekly with folded arms.

"Abou Nassar," said the *charge d'affaires*, still speaking in English, "write."

The youth bowed, seated himself at a little table, and drew forth pad-block and fountain pen.

"Dictate to my secretary," said Tufik to the waiting Brenner, "the form of receipt you desire."

"Received from Galvin Brenner, in good condition, the original Amina rug," dictated Brenner.

"Sign it with my name and affix to it the embassy seal," Tufik commanded the secretary, adding to himself:

"If this man erases the rest of the writing and forges a draft with my name at the foot, the name in Halil's handwriting shall avail him little at the banks."

Brenner took the sealed receipt from the secretary's hand, folded it, and put it in his pocket.

"That's all," he said briskly. "I hope I haven't kept you too long and made you late for your appointment, whatever it is. I'll have just time to catch the 8.30 for New York."

The secretary, at a sign from Tufik, had reverently picked up the rug, and now bore it from the room.

Nor did the eye of a foreigner again rest upon the Amina until, a month later, it was restored to its place of honor in the great mosque.

The treasure safe, Tufik Khan turned his fuller attention to the strange American who had still more strangely delivered the rug to him. The Persian's curiosity was whetted to razor edge.

"Will you not tell me," he asked courteously, "how you chanced to—to find the Amina?"

"My friend," countered Brenner with equal suavity, "when you are a guest at a well-appointed dinner, do you ask your host how he chanced to find the money to pay for it? You wanted the rug. I brought it to you. That is all. Make for yourself what capital you choose out of the recovery when you send it back to your government. My part of the show is over."

"But there are rewards—honors—preferments—for the—"

"For the man who wants them. I don't care to profit by the return of stolen goods."

"But an explanation surely is due."

"It will stay overdue, then. Of course you might detain me on some such charge as housebreaking and try to get the facts that way. But you'll hardly do it. Too much would have to be made public. Good night."

Before the dumfounded Persian could frame a new question Brenner had bowed, turned on his heel, and passed out.

"I think," he mused as he went, "that closes the incident."

But, oddly enough, it did not.

CHAPTER XVIII.

One More Bargain.

GALVIN BRENNER, ESQ.
    SIR:
        If you will call upon me at the above address to-morrow morning, between 9 and 9.15, it may be to your advantage.
        Very truly, CLYDE IRWIN.
            (Per P. H.)

The "above address" was General Irwin's house, not his office. And the note was lying beside Brenner's plate when he came down to a somewhat late breakfast at his boarding-house on the morning after his return from Washington.

He read the brief epistle, looked at his watch, saw that the hour was 8.30, then settled back to a leisurely breakfast.

He felt there was no need of haste.

Indeed, he was of two minds whether or not to obey the summons. He could not see how it would be of advantage to himself in any way.

He knew perfectly well why the great financier had sent for him. Also how Irwin chanced to know his name and address.

Ulrich Laing, in reporting failure to deliver the rug, had of course told the general the whole story. And Irwin, supposing Brenner was holding the rug as a personal speculation, was probably sending for him with an idea of making terms.

Though there was no longer anything over which such terms could be made, yet a spirit of mischief at length decided Brenner to accede to the demand for an interview.

It might prove amusing. And it would not long detain him from his quest for a new job.

He had already resolved to devote the day—and so many more days as it might require—to finding work. The restoration of the rug, he told himself, had done much to wipe clean his past misdeeds.

It was nearly half past nine when Brenner reached General Clyde Irwin's big house in "Millionaires' Row."

This time he rang at the front door instead of at the servants' entrance. And no less personage than the butler answered the bell.

That portly functionary fairly swelled with indignant superiority as he recognized the former "electric light inspector."

Brenner cut short any hesitancy by presenting General Irwin's note. The butler read it superciliously and, deigning no comment, led the way into the house and into a small reception-room. Then he vanished, to return in a minute with the lofty tidings:

"General Irwin will see you in the library."

He led the way once more, this time up a flight of stairs and to an open, portièred door.

Drawing aside the curtain, he announced:

"Mr. Brenner!"

He managing to instil into his perfectly and tonelessly correct voice a world of covert disdain.

Brenner walked into a high wainscoted room, rich, dark, and very simple in its general effect.

In a leather chair near a bay window sat a tall, lean man whose head was crowned by a veritable mop of snow-white hair. The face beneath was keen, strong, almost expressionless.

From dozens of newspaper pictures Brenner at once recognized the tall man as General Clyde Irwin—mighty power on Wall Street and international finance, and well known as one of America's most notable art collectors.

Brenner stepped into the room and came to a stop near the door. Irwin raised a pair of tired, heavy-lidded eyes at the other's advent.

He cast a single slow, appraising glance at Brenner, then turned as if not at all interested in what he saw, and resumed his reading of the morning paper.

Brenner noted the studied slight, and he flushed. But he said quietly:

"I am Galvin Brenner. You wrote that you wished to see me this morning."

"Between 9 and 9.15," rasped the general. "It is now half past nine. I am not used to being kept waiting like an errand boy. I don't think I care to see you to-day."

"As you like," pleasantly assented Brenner, turning to walk out.

"Wait!" called Irwin in some surprise. "Come back. Why weren't you here when I told you to be?"

"First, because I got back very late from Washington and overslept. Second, because I am not under your orders."

There was neither flippancy nor ill-temper in the tone of the retort.

Irwin looked a second time from under his heavy-lidded eyes at the man who so unconcernedly refused to cringe, as did most of the general's humble associates.

"Sit down," he grunted.

Brenner chose a comfortable chair and seated himself—not on its edge, but far back in it.

"Where's the Amina?" demanded Irwin.

"With the people it belongs to," was the quiet response.

"Didn't bring it along, eh?"

"Obviously not."

There was a little pause. Then Irwin said, coming hard to the point.

"Laing told me all about it yesterday afternoon. Said you'd gotten the rug back, then overpowered him when you learned how valuable the Amina is, and ran away with it."

"Quite true."

"You must be courting another term in state prison."

"I have never been in state prison," corrected Brenner gently, "any more than you have. Perhaps we've both been lucky beyond our deserts; you in high finance, I in pettier theft.

"And this time I'm not going to prison, either. For if I did I might have to take with me two men whom society could ill spare."

"Laing tells me you're a crook. A common thief."

"Except for a mistake in tense, he is right. I *was* a crook. But a rather uncommon thief. I am neither any more."

"The whining penitent, eh? "

"If you like," acquiesced Brenner with no shadow of offense at the slur.

"You seem to be making several false starts."

"I may in future. Up to now I've made but one. And last night I retrieved that."

"I want the Amina rug."

"So Mr. Laing told me," said Brenner, "but I'm afraid you'll never get it."

"Money will buy most things."

"It will buy a large assortment," answered Brenner, "but I'm afraid that rug is no longer on the list."

"Good!" grudgingly assented the general. "I was afraid you were going to make the canting speech of the reformed about money not buying peace of mind."

"I've had too little experience with either to know which will buy which," laughed Brenner. "As to the rug—"

"What's your price?" snapped Irwin.

"I haven't the rug."

"Don't lie to me. You took it from Laing yesterday."

"Lying is not one of my pretty tricks, general. But I beg you won't

keep me remembering all the time that you are an old man and that I am not.

"It is true I took the rug from Mr. Laing, to prevent him from selling it to you, after he and you had had it stolen from a place of worship and had been made a catspaw to steal it again. I took it. And I had it sent back to Persia."

"*What?*" roared the incredulous general.

For answer Brenner drew out the receipt signed by Tufik Khan's secretary and handed it to Irwin.

The general took it, read it, wide-eyed, then read it over again and turned it sidewise to examine the seal.

After which the document fluttered to the floor and the old man stared agape at Brenner.

"You're more than a crook," he vouchsafed at last. "You're a financier. You found the reward offered by Persia was bigger than my price. But you might have made still more by giving me another chance to bid."

"I didn't ask for a reward. I didn't get one."

"Don't carry a joke too far!" scoffed Irwin.

Brenner shrugged his shoulders. And Irwin, scanning his face, exclaimed:

"Lord! The man's telling the truth!"

"A habit I picked up as a boy," apologized Brenner.

General Irwin did not answer. He was still eying the younger man with a curious intentness. And into the shrewd old face had crept a kindlier, more human light.

After a long silence the general said in a new voice:

"Do you mind telling me the whole story? From your first visit to Laing up to the way you got the receipt from the Persian *charge d'affairs?* And, first, will you accept my apology for speaking to you as I did? I am sorry."

There was something in Irwin's tone or words that struck close to Brenner's heart and that loosened his tongue.

Briefly, concisely, yet with a vividness that was unconscious, he told his story.

He sketched his early career, his longing for a clean life, his experience with Laing and the forty Ali Babas, the finding of the Amina at Irwin's own house, and the later scene in Laing's office.

Then he went on to tell of his visit to Washington.

General Irwin did not interrupt. His face did not change, nor did his eyes once leave the speaker's.

And when the brief tale was done he spoke no word.

"That is all," finished Brenner, getting to his feet, "I am afraid I have taken far too much of a busy man's time with my rambling yarn. And now I must go."

"Where? "

"This is my job-hunting day."

"This is your job-finding day, if you choose to make it so. Do you want to come to work for me, Mr. Brenner? A comfortable living wage at the start? Then advancement as fast as you make good—and from what I know of you, I think you'll waste mighty little time in making good."

"But," stammered Brenner, "I know nothing of finance. I should be a bad investment for you. I've had no training along that line."

"You've had a lifelong training along certain popular branches of that line," corrected Irwin, smiling a little.

Then, more seriously, the general went on.

"In Wall Street—in the railroad world—in the world of strong men, and hard battle—there is one type of employee for whom the demand always so far exceeds the supply that such an employee can command big pay from the very start.

"I refer to the man who is alert, resourceful, tireless, free from fear or favor, and who dares to be honest even to his own hurt and will risk loss for the sake of his principles. The man whose soul the fire has tempered, not withered. The employer who gets that type of man is getting a treasure better than any Amina rug.

"And *you* are such a man, Mr. Galvin Brenner. Will you come to work for me—to-day? "

"Yes!" cried Brenner. "*Yes!*"

(The end.)

Human Interest Stuff

A graphic narrative adaptation of the short story from *A Terhune Omnibus*, illustrated by long-time professional comics artist William Messner-Loebs.

Available on eBay.

Will Eisner always said that Bill Loebs was the closest to his own drawing style and story-telling methodology, among Will's many acolytes, in whose number I proudly count myself. "Human Interest Stuff" establishes that Bill can still hit and sustain that exalted high artistic note, adapted from Terhune's deeply affecting short story, with gifted collaborator Rodney Schroeter. It's like having Will back with us again. Bravo!

Dave Sim

I do think you've picked up on the flavor of the Albert Payson Terhune story.

Marilyn R. Horowitz

Rodney Schroeter has delivered a smart script, a page-turner, a winner by every yard-stick. Best of all, he was clever enough to recruit Bill Messner-Loebs as his artist, so you have to stop and stare at every panel. "Human Interest Stuff" is the dope.

Clifford Meth

Rodney Schroeter and William Messner-Loebs have revived that time-honored but half-forgotten pulp subgenre, the sentimental dog story. You will never forget Tatters!

Will Murray

I don't suspect I've read a comic book since I was 12 years old—but as they say, sometimes you need to stuff your old ideas and ways of doing things aside and look at something in a new light.

Well, was I ever surprised. The story starts out with action and it just keeps right on truckin' along, keeping the reader, looker, or whatever you call a comic book consumer right on the edge of his chair wondering what's about to happen next.

This is a fine story, no question about it. Makes a good point, in fact several of them. I like the way the story is organized, and I like the way it takes a few twists and turns. Oh, I also like that even the threat of the pen can make some folks squirm a bit—and sometimes do what's right.

Jerry Apps

Once upon a time the comics were fresh, original, emotional, exciting, timely and timeless, interesting, romantic and memorable.

"Human Interest Stuff" is the type of story that attracted and attracts me to the comics.

Rodney Schroeter and William Messner-Loebs deserve a 21-gun salute.

Because.

Once upon a time is now.

Robin Snyder